BICYCLES & BROOMSTICKS

FANTASTICAL FEMINIST STORIES ABOUT WITCHES ON BIKES

EDITED BY

ELLY BLUE

ELLY BLUE PUBLISHING,
AN IMPRINT OF MICROCOSM PUBLISHING
PORTLAND, OR

BICYCLES & BROOMSTICKS
FANTASTICAL FEMINIST STORIES ABOUT WITCHES ON BIKES

Edited by Elly Blue
All content © its creators, 2023
Final editorial content © Elly Blue, 2023
This edition © Elly Blue Publishing, an imprint of Microcosm Publishing, 2023
First printing, January 10, 2023
All work remains the property of the original creators.

ISBN 9781648411304
This is Microcosm #708

Elly Blue Publishing, an imprint of Microcosm Publishing
2752 N Williams Ave.
Portland, OR 97227
https://microcosm.pub/BikesInSpace

Cover art by Gerta Egy
Design by Joe Biel

Thank you to Lydia Rogue, Ru Mehendale, Marley Schlichting, Rose Marshall, and Jennifer Lee Rossman for invaluable editorial support.

Elly Blue Publishing, an imprint of Microcosm Publishing
2752 N Williams Ave
Portland, OR 97227

This is Bikes in Space Volume 9
For more volumes visit BikesInSpace.com
For more feminist bicycle books and zines visit TakingTheLane.com

MICROCOSM · PUBLISHING

ABOUT THE PUBLISHER

ELLY BLUE PUBLISHING was founded in 2010 to focus on feminist fiction and nonfiction about bicycling. In 2015, Elly Blue Publishing merged to become an imprint of Microcosm Publishing that is still fully managed by Elly Blue.

MICROCOSM PUBLISHING is Portland's most diversified publishing house and distributor with a focus on the colorful, authentic, and empowering. Our books and zines have put your power in your hands since 1996, equipping readers to make positive changes in their lives and in the world around them. Microcosm emphasizes skill-building, showing hidden histories, and fostering creativity through challenging conventional publishing wisdom with books and bookettes about DIY skills, food, bicycling, gender, self-care, and social justice. What was once a distro and record label started by Joe Biel in a drafty bedroom was selected as *Publisher's Weekly's* fastest growing publisher of 2022 and has become among the oldest independent publishing houses in Portland, OR and Cleveland, OH. We are a politically moderate, centrist publisher in a world that has inched to the right for the past 80 years.

Global labor conditions are bad, and our roots in industrial Cleveland in the 70s and 80s made us appreciate the need to treat workers right. Therefore, our books are MADE IN THE USA

[TABLE OF CONTENTS]

INTRODUCTION TO THE 2237 EDITION

Since the Great Plague took all the magic from us, the galaxy has been a cold and lonely place, with humans reliant on faulty and fallible machines to transport us, shade us from radiation, and even facilitate our communication and entertainment.

It is up to us archivists to look to the stories of Earth's pre-magical past. Looking back to when the vast loneliness of the universe and the fraught results of our own technology were even more pressing issues can help us to see how people imagined their future so that we too can find hope again.

Many stories survive of this time when most people had no access to magic, and the few who could capture a glimmering of it were persecuted and villainized. The Great Awakening normalized and honed our magical capabilities, allowing us to settle throughout the galaxy and to live without the destructive tendencies and technologies of the times before. But this golden age ended after barely a century, when the Plague came and burned that nascent magic back into a mere trickle.

Our magic now must lie in our stories, our dreams, and our care for our communities past, present, and future. We remember our brief era of glorious undertaking and expansion with nostalgic pride, but we also remember who we were before. Instead of seeing our ancestors as limited and primitive, we must now view them as role models.

It is with this ancestral respect and curiosity in mind that we republish this volume of stories, found in a personal archive and clearly intended for publication. The ten stories and introduction show multiple things of historical value:

- The specific cultural constraints of the time they were written, which appears to be shortly before the Great Awakening. Clearly magic was conceived of as mythical yet desirable, dangerous yet worthy of defense. In the most realistic stories it is taken as a matter of spiritual engagement, and only the sillier imaginings offer theories of magic that can materially affect the universe.

- These stories reimagine the past and present as well as the future and alternate universes. Clearly the authors' and editor's goal is similar to ours—questing inward and outward for meaning in a time of uncertainty.

- The use of the archaic term "feminism" in the collection title is harder to explain to a modern audience. Many treatises have been written about this ancient reliance on a binary system of "gender" that was decided at birth and expected to determine an individual's identity and societal role throughout their life. It's a fascinating relic we can take much caution from studying. You can see through the use of the more modern "they," rather than the old fashioned "she" and "he," in many of the stories and author biographies that the concept of gender was beginning to fall out of vogue around the time of writing— another moment in history that social historians make much of but bears little relevance to most of us today.

- Our team of archivists has combed the records in preparation for the release of this volume to explain another, even more baffling, of its core themes: the "bicycle." It seems this was initially a machine powered by human exertion magnified by a system of gears, though powered versions existed as well. It was intended for land transport, primarily on asphalt-paved roads, and primarily used as an individual vehicle for solo transportation or carrying cargo and passengers short distances, and was also used as a sporting device in speed and endurance competitions. The goal of including the "bicycle" element alongside the "feminist" element in this collection of stories appears to be an attempt to connect what the editor saw to be the liberatory capacity of both against a common enemy they termed "the petropatriarchy." Whether or not it is valid to directly connect gender-based inequities with the economic inequities fueled by the energy-based economy of the time is a matter for historians to debate, but we wouldn't count it out.

We can't help but cheer on the optimism of these writers (and, presumably, their intended audience), in hoping not just for a more equitable world, but for one less reliant on the fossil fuels and the resulting climate disasters that caused such upheaval at that time. Perhaps it was this same optimism that sparked the outward movement from Earth after the Awakening, in addition to the rehabilitative efforts planetside that continue, although more slowly and with greater difficulty unaided by magic, to this day.

The real value to these stories is not to settle academic debates about the past, but to get inside the minds and the imaginations of the non-magic users who came before us, from whom we have so much to re-learn about everyday, magicless human life. May they rest in peace—we thank them for all they have shared with us.

INTRODUCTION TO THE 2023 EDITION

I learned to read because of the Wicked Witch of the West. I was three and I was obsessed with the *Wizard of Oz*, demanding repeated, back-to-back readings to the point that I had the book memorized. The Witch, from her confident navigation of a tornado on her rickety bicycle to her ultimate downfall in a puddle of water, frightened me and captured my imagination. It wasn't just Miss Almira Gulch; I generally over-identified with the villains in stories. So discovering the redemption of witches in fractured fairy tales, feminist histories, and modern paganism as a teen came as soul-level relief.

When I chose the theme for this volume, I hoped that it would bring out a wide range of interpretations, and I was definitely not disappointed. In these ten stories, we have contemporary neo-pagans, fantasy worlds inhabited by magical creatures, an 1890s midwife, an occultist and wheelwoman of a similar era, and other spellcasters in totally unique settings, from the earnest to the comedic.

A surprise theme emerged (one always does)—of resilience and healing. From the opening story of a resilience spell to the the final story's hilarious redemption of moving house by bike, and much of what's in between: bicycles are, in these stories, a sort of spell, cast for a safe haven in a witch's messy office, a reprieve from profound loneliness, a way to heal a broken household, a forest clearing, and a city beset with magical smog, and even the heart of a robot.

So that's nice to see further redemption of witch archetypes.

Speaking of themes, I've been thinking for a while about changing the tagline for the series from "feminist" to "queer." The former word's so deeply loaded with over a century of hostile takeovers and exclusionary tactics. It's unsurprising when it's used as a slur, or taken on as a meaningless rallying cry to buy consumer goods. But who knew that the term "radical feminist" would come in recent years to stand for such violently anti-woman bigotry? I'm not ready to admit defeat and give the word up to any of those forces.

At an event years ago, I was passing out "feminists against freeways" stickers, enjoying the variety of responses. "We have to be against cars now, too?" said one woman who took one with great, resigned weariness. I stammered in confusion, but it's a clear encapsulation of the difficulty with the word. The idea that in order to be feminist you need to agree with all other feminists, or fundamentally share every platform is baked in... yet it's so completely counterproductive to building a widespread movement. Or maybe the point is that it's the engine of building an exclusionary movement where only the agendas of the people with the most powerful voices count.

For the purposes of these volumes, I take "feminist" to encompass plenty of complexity. Boiled down to its simplest form, "not sexist" is the best definition I could come up with at the outset. Today it seems important to add "not gender-essentialist." The fields of science fiction and fantasy have opened up spectacularly in the decade that I've been publishing these volumes, but are still wracked by entrenched stereotypes of macho spacemen and helpless women (if women appear in the story at all), the chosen prince and the vixen who tries to thwart him or the maiden he gets to rescue, etc. Classically, any woman with power or who isn't primarily defined by beauty must be a villain, or a witch.

So that's the baseline. But the deeper that questioning of norms and stereotypes goes, the better. I'll publish a story centering menstruation, pregnancy, or abortion, but nobody needs to have a uterus for the story to be feminist. A perfectly functional submission for this volume simply has a woman, trans, and/or nonbinary main character, or doesn't specify the protagonist's gender, and that protagonist isn't unreflexively defined by their relationships with men. My favorite stories either subtly or overtly play with gender norms, and really, the queerer the better for these volumes. But the bar for feminism here is pretty low—which doesn't stop a number of submitters every year from failing to clear it.

The bar's a bit higher for the bicycle element... I ask contributors to make bikes essential to the plot, but I'll let a bicycle-shaped MacGuffin slip through sometimes for a story I love. My favorite stories are framed in resistance to transportation and energy norms as well as gender norms. I love the word "petropatriarchy," which sums up so much of what these books seek to reimagine.

Back to witchcraft . . . I think you'll fall in love with the practitioners in these stories as they struggle to heal themselves, their communities, their worlds, and random kids who show up at their doorstop. Sometimes that means a quiet moment with a crystal or a madcap ride through the city; other times it means turning your opponents into toasters. Whatever healing and resilience mean to you, I hope you find what you need of it in the coming year. In the meantime, please enjoy this book!

Elly Blue

Portland, Oregon

August, 2022

OLD GOLIATH
✌ Emily Burton ✌

There is a point in adolescence when most young girls embark on a kind of cycle. For my human friend Marietta, this cycle involved hiding menstrual pads up her sleeves. For my cousin Laila, it meant dragging mauled bodies into her parents' garage every full moon (we're still working on that).

For me, cycling meant learning to ride a bike. Specifically, learning to ride Old Goliath.

Old Goliath was an ancient mountain bike, barely holding it together after twenty-odd years traveling across the Pacific Northwest. With its adventuring years now behind it, it leaned rustily against the raised-bed gardens in our backyard, remaining upright only with the aid of Mom's resiliency charm. It stayed in that position for the first twelve years of my life. I spent my childhood perched on its seat, watching Mom sow sunflower seeds and unearth bright purple beetroots from the rich soil of our backyard. Memories of Old Goliath mixed together with memories of my mother: the smell of her perfume, the scratchy wool of her sweaters, the leathery touch of her gardening glove against my cheek.

I stopped resting in the garden with Old Goliath when Mom passed away. Sometimes memories are too painful to relive; sometimes it's easier to forget them all at once.

Grandma didn't think so, though. There's a well-known adage which states that old people grow to look like their pets over time, fluffing up like standard poodles or turning droopy like ancient basset hounds. Thing is, Grandma didn't age to resemble her hairless cat, Snuggles, or the lizards that ran amuck behind the old folks home. Instead, she steadily became more and more like an elephant. Grandma remembered *everything* and she stored it all between her two enormous ears.

Three days after Mom's funeral, Grandma moved into our dilapidated little house on Redwood Street. She needed no tour of the place; she'd lived with us when I was a baby and she still remembered every loose floorboard and creaking step. Most importantly, she remembered the box she'd left behind twelve years ago, when Mom had deemed herself capable enough to raise me alone. It had stayed there, stored away in the attic and seemingly forgotten for all this time. Except, of course, that Grandma never forgot anything.

She sent me up to the attic on a sunny autumn Saturday, with directions to bring down an old cardboard box filled to the brim with spellbooks. I set the box down on the kitchen table with a resounding *thud* and Grandma nodded smugly.

"You, my dear Athena," she declared, "have some studying to do."

If Grandma meant to distract me from my grief, she certainly provided more than enough opportunities. My mother had been a patient tutor, walking me through the occasional untangling charm or quick-fix spell as needed. There was nothing patient about Grandma, though: she turned my bedroom floor into a veritable maze of grimoires, and our whole house into a hazard zone of flying plates, self-lighting hearths, and talking wallpaper. Every hour after school was filled with charms demonstrations, potion-making, and defensive maneuvers. Grandma could turn just about anything into a magical how-to lesson, from baking cookies to banishing wasps from the backyard.

Four months passed in a blur of incantations. Then, one winter afternoon, she suggested I learn a spell from my mother's childhood grimoire.

"Ella kept her grimoire as a kind of diary when she was your age," she said gently. She placed a spiral-bound notebook in my outstretched hands.

Mom's grimoire was nothing like the ancient leather books in Grandma's collection. Looped writing and scribbled hearts dominated its shiny purple cover, left behind by glitter pens and permanent markers. Left behind by my mother.

I flipped the notebook open, blinking away tears to read the spells scrawled in the margins of every page: recipes for acne and hair removal, step-by-step directions for mixing love potions, and there—on page sixty-five—the words to a resiliency charm. *Old Goliath*'s resiliency charm.

"I want to learn this one." I held the notebook out to Grandma, pointing to the spell written in cursive under a section about cursing Algebra teachers.

"A resiliency charm." Grandma raised a penciled-in eyebrow at me, crossing her heavily-bangled arms over her chest. "You're twelve years old, Athena. What could you possibly need a resiliency charm for? Your sore old back?"

I scowled at her, sinking into the chair across from hers at the kitchen table. I ran my fingers along a gouge in the table, left behind by one of Mom's enchanted chopping knives. My eyes stung as if it still floated there, cutting onions under her watchful gaze.

"I just want to learn it, okay?"

"Well, alright then," Grandma said, nodding resolutely. She ran a finger over one of the doodles in Mom's grimoire, this time of a bicycle with biceps.

"That's it?" I asked.

"That's it." She dusted her hands off on her long paisley apron, motioning for me to join her in the garden. "Best not to start with human trials. If I remember correctly, your mom used to practice on my old mountain bike."

I startled, nearly falling off my chair. "Old Goliath was your bike?"

"One and the same."

I stared at Grandma as she crossed the kitchen to the back door and jammed her big feet into even bigger Wellies.

She looked at me impatiently. "Are you coming, kiddo?"

I nodded mutely as she slipped out the door and into the backyard.

Grandma's old bike. I'd always assumed Old Goliath was Mom's—she'd told me so many stories about her travels across Oregon and Washington, how she'd zoomed past giant redwood trees and enchanted the bike to fly on cloudy days.

Picturing Grandma on Old Goliath was *a lot* harder. She wasn't tough the same way Mom was: even in our old photo albums, Grandma always had little gold-rimmed glasses and big, poofy white hair. I couldn't remember ever seeing her without her signature flowing dresses and worn-out aprons.

Still, I followed her into the backyard, determined to learn Mom's resiliency charm.

"There you are." Grandma waved me over to where she stood between two raised-bed gardens, hidden from the waist-down by one of the tall wooden boxes. Old Goliath leaned pitifully against the other bed, its handlebars rusted and its paint job peeling from the rain.

Guilt swirled in my chest, but I pushed it away. It had only been a few months since Mom had last checked in on the garden. The old bike had survived worse, hadn't it?

"Now, your mother wrote a lot of spells in her time," Grandma said firmly, "but this one requires a particular strength. You have to be the boss of the bike. Got it?" I nodded, even though I very much did *not* get it.

"Old Goliath here has been chugging along since I was a girl—so that's, hmmm. Let's not put a number on that one, actually. Let's just say, Ol' Goliath's got some years under its belt drive."

Grandma patted the worn leather seat. "Hop on then."

I balked, almost falling backward into a barren gladiolus bed. "Why?"

Grandma frowned, pushing up her glasses with one hand. "How else will you know what needs restoring, dear? The best way to learn Old Goliath's weak-points is to ride it." Tears pricked the backs of my eyes, hot and sharp. "No," I said firmly.

"No?" Grandma scowled at my tone, but her face softened as she took in my trembling lower lip. "Oh," she sighed. "Oh dear."

I frowned, swiping at the moisture in my eyes. I'd grown used to the look in Grandma's beady eyes, recognized it from the faces of my classmates and teachers. *Pity.* I was an orphan and, worse than that, I was an orphan who didn't know how to ride a stupid bike.

"Mom was going to teach me," I snapped, even though Grandma hadn't asked. "She said I could learn whenever I wanted. I was going to—I was going to learn—"

But Old Goliath always looked so rickety and rusted, as if it could fall apart at any moment. And, anyway, I was so comfortable sitting on its stationary seat, leaning safely against the warm wood of the raised-bed gardens while Mom weeded beside me.

But now Mom was gone and Old Goliath was still rusted and rickety and frozen in place.

Grandma's voice interrupted my thoughts, gentle and warm.

"Let's take the day off," she suggested. I looked up to see her smiling at me from beside Old Goliath, her arm wrapped around its body as if it, too, was a beloved grandchild. "There's more to life than magic, Athena. Go change into some proper shoes while I fix up the dangerous bits. I'll meet you by the front door."

I had never expected my grandmother to say anything against magic and I stayed in a kind of shocked state as we drove to a forest near the edge of the town.

But she repeated those words again as she stood at the mouth of a bike path, one hand placed obstinately on each hip. "There's more to life than magic," she said firmly. "You won't be using any today."

"What?" I gaped at her in disbelief. "Why not?"

Grandma raised an eyebrow at me. "I learned to ride this bike without magic and your mother did too, so that's what you're going to do. You have to experience some things for yourself."

Old Goliath stood between us, its metal body wavering slightly in the breeze. To be fair, it looked less rickety than I'd ever seen it, the wheels and handlebars shining with new life from Grandma's spellcasting. Still, I figured it wouldn't make much difference how pretty the bike was if I was staring up at it from the ground.

"What about a protection spell?" I bargained, peering hopefully up at Grandma.

She answered by dumping a helmet into my arms.

"There's your protection spell," she said. "Off you go. I'll send something along to help you."

I scowled at her, but I grabbed Old Goliath by the handlebars and dragged it resolutely down the bike path. Admittedly, Grandma had picked a beautiful area for me to wipe out in. The path was lined with giant redwoods and smaller pine trees, and the air smelled deliciously like Christmas. I wondered how badly I'd have to injure myself for Grandma to make me her famous gingerbread cookies.

I walked about a half-mile down the path, wondering how far she wanted me to go. The forest grew progressively darker as I went along, the canopy thickening overhead with whispering green leaves.

Suddenly there was a bang and a flash and, a few feet in front of me, an image of my grandmother puffed into existence. Except I could tell from the flickering of her body and the smoothness of her skin that this was not the Grandma I knew.

I leaned cautiously against Old Goliath as the memory spell played out down the road. Grandma—younger despite her puffy white hair and glasses—dragged a reluctant little girl down the tree-lined path before me. My chest tightened as I recognized my mother, five-years-old and scowling behind a cloud of curly red hair. She looked pouty and peevish and so ... *alive.* I leaned more heavily against Old Goliath, half-expecting it to collapse under me. It didn't.

"But I don't *want* to ride that bike!" she snapped at Grandma. "I want the *pink* one from the *store!*"

"Well, this is the one you have," Grandma said cheerfully. She scooped Mom up and placed her on Old Goliath's seat, and then plopped a familiar blue helmet onto her head. It fell over Mom's face, covering her eyes and bopping her on the nose.

I touched the velcro strap at my own chin and a smile tugged at the corners of my mouth, unfamiliar and a little heavy, but not wrong.

Grandma chuckled and performed a quick resizing spell on Mom's helmet while she squirmed irritably.

"Take a deep breath," Grandma instructed. Her holographic figure turned toward me with an expectant expression and I was pulled back to reality with a jolt.

I sucked in a shaky gulp of air. The fuzzy image of Grandma nodded smugly.

"Good," she said, turning back to my mother. "Now it's your turn, Ella."

"What do you mean *my* turn? There's no one else even here," my mom responded sourly. But she breathed in noisily and waited for further instructions.

Grandma walked us through the motions of riding Old Goliath. Together with my five-year-old mother, I learned to balance my feet on its pedals and bike wobbly circles around the fuzzy memory spell.

After a short lesson, Mom grew bored of Grandma's instructions.

"I'm ready!" she insisted, leaning forward over the handlebars eagerly. "Can I go or what?"

Grandma laughed, a deep, throaty sound I hadn't heard since before Mom died.

"Go!" Grandma cried.

Mom set off at a rapid pace, pedaling furiously down the path. I hurried to orient myself on Old Goliath. With one more breath, I shoved my feet into the pedal straps and dashed off after her.

We biked side-by-side down the rocky dirt road, our faces flushing in unison and our wild red hair flying along behind us.

At some point, the flickering image faded. My mother faded with it, until I was alone in the forest, following a solitary path between giant redwood trees and sweet-smelling pines. Still, somehow, I didn't want to stop. I closed my eyes against the sound of the wind whipping through the trees and breathed long and deep. I knew, when I opened my eyes again, that the image of Mom would be gone. My lungs clenched as I remembered that last, fading glimpse of her, but I breathed through it. I *could* breathe through it.

Snap! At last, my eyes opened as a camera flashed from a few yards away. Grandma stood at the mouth of the forest, waving wildly at me with a polaroid camera in her hand. I grinned at her, and then grinned wider as a gust of wind rushed into my open mouth. It soared down my throat and I swallowed it in quick, eager gasps.

When I finally came to a stop and slipped down off Old Goliath, Grandma handed me the polaroid she had taken. I watched as it developed in my palm, the image flickering slowly into view.

A girl with flushed cheeks and bright eyes flew down a tree-lined path, grinning as her red hair billowed out behind her.

"You look just like your mother here," Grandma whispered, her voice catching.

We smiled down at the photograph together, sharing the same memory. A few minutes passed before we managed to look away and turn towards the path forward. When we did, we led Old Goliath back to the car together, each of us gripping one rusted blue handlebar. I held onto the polaroid, too—there was a place waiting for it in our family photo album, next to another photograph of a little girl on a bicycle.

In that moment, as the two of us held up that old, ramshackle bike, carrying those memories didn't seem quite so impossible either.

LAYINGS OUT AND LYINGS IN
ᦉ *Kathleen Jowitt* ᦉ

The church clock struck two, and the moon broke through a gap in the clouds. For a moment it illuminated the narrow street, the cottages on either side, and the two people who had just emerged from two different doors.

The man raised his shallow hat. "Good evening, Mrs. Banks. Or I suppose I should say, good morning."

He spoke quietly. So did she. "And the same to you, Reverend." Her smile was just visible, though the darkness and her old-fashioned coal-scuttle bonnet did their best to obscure it. She nodded over her shoulder, indicating the door from which she had just come. "You'll have a christening to do soon."

"That's excellent news. Is all—er—well there?"

"She'll do nicely, and so will the baby."

"I'm glad of it." Now it was the vicar who looked back to where he had come from. "I'm afraid you'll be wanted at the Austins' before too long."

She lowered her voice yet further. "Gaffer Jack? He's done well to last the winter. I hope it doesn't hurt him too much."

"He seems as easy as might be hoped. I was able to offer him some comfort."

"Good."

"May I offer you a lift home, Mrs. Banks? I have the gig."

She made a little dip. "I'm grateful for the offer, Reverend, but I have my own conveyance waiting for me." She gestured at the black-painted, two-wheeled machine propped against the wall. "I'll be home in no time."

"Good heavens," he said. "It looks rather, ah, undignified."

She grinned. "Could be worse; at least it's a 'safety' model. It's more comfortable than you'd think, too, to look at it. I've no doubt you'll be riding one yourself in a year or so." She stifled a yawn. "Well, good night, Reverend."

"Good night, Mrs. Banks."

She bobbed; he bowed. Out of consideration for the young man's delicate sensibilities, Aggie Banks wheeled the machine down the street until vicar and horse and gig had passed her; then she hoisted her skirts up, swung her right leg over the crossbar, and set off towards home.

Her bonnet strings streamed out behind her in the breeze as she pedalled through the quiet streets. It jolted somewhat over the stones. She had heard that the larger wheels of the penny-farthings made for a more comfortable ride, but she had neither the height nor the youthful agility to mount one of those monsters; and besides, it would have been a little eccentric, even for Aggie Banks. She liked the symmetry of the wheels and the sinuous lines of the frame of this one, anyway. Sarah had scolded her for blowing her savings on such a newfangled device ("and at your age, too!"), but Aggie had assured her that it would pay for itself in no time.

The machine had allowed her to come out further than usual this evening. Tilford had been a village for a very long time, but now that it had a railway station it was fast becoming a town. Still, a distance that would have taken her a painful three quarters of an hour on foot was barely ten minutes on the bicycle. She could be doing lyings-in for another thirty years.

Once home, she took the usual precautions before leaving the bicycle in the shed and scuttling quietly to the back door. She did not trouble to light a candle: at the age of fifty-five, her sight was as clear as it had been at twenty, and almost as good in the dark as it was in the daylight. She undressed swiftly, leaving her clothes draped over the back of a chair.

Sarah was asleep, but she stirred when Aggie turned down the blankets and slipped in next to her.

"Aggie," she murmured. "Your feet are cold." But she rolled over and snuggled up against her, nonetheless.

℘ • ℘

The chill of February gave way to a wet March, a combination of circumstances that hastened the end for many of the old and infirm of Tilford. Both women were kept occupied with the business of the dead. Each body had to be washed, its eyes closed, hair combed, and arms crossed over the chest.

Aggie got soaked to the skin on the way home from laying out Harry Brimcombe, and caught a chill. Sarah told her that this ought to have been an obvious consequence of going out in the rain without an overcoat, even to those *not* blessed with the gift of foresight. Aggie was too miserable even to snap at her, and remained meekly in bed for the best part of thirty-six hours.

Sarah, therefore, was considerably alarmed when she returned from a birth (Kate Mulford's fifth, which had arrived at four o'clock in the afternoon with minimal assistance) to find Aggie out of bed and pulling on a dress over her nightgown.

"Aggie—what do you think you're doing?" Sarah unfastened her cloak.

Aggie turned to look at her. Her face was blank and her eyes seemed clouded.

Sarah knew this look. Her heart clenched. "What is it?"

"Rosie Crowthorne."

Yes, Sarah supposed, that was to be expected. Had she been called upon to make a prediction, she might have given Rosie another week, but she would not have put money on it. "It's going to be a difficult one?"

Aggie groped under the bed for her boots. "Better be there."

She sat down on the bed next to her. "No, you daft old bag, I'll go."

"Then you'll take my bicycle. I mean it. She'll need you sooner than you can get there on foot."

"Why? What will I need?" She knew it was useless even as she said it. Very rarely did Aggie's foresight provide her with clear details of what was to pass. Most often, as now, it came as a simple sense of urgency.

Aggie only shook her head, setting her grey hair flying, and said, again, "The bicycle."

"I'm not setting foot on that contraption of yours at my time of life."

"It'll cause less comment than a broomstick. But if you don't want to go . . ." Aggie pulled her boots on and began to fasten the laces.

"I'll go, I'll go." Sarah took her cloak up once again. "How do I ride the thing, then?"

Aggie grinned. "Very much like a broomstick, as it happens. Just swing your leg over it and push off."

"Less of your cheek. And I'll thank you to go back to bed." Quite apart from anything else, Sarah had no desire to have Aggie watch her first attempt to ride a bicycle.

↬ • ↫

In fact, it rode very much more like a broomstick than she had expected. Once she had adjusted her stance to compensate for the additional height, and got used to the continual rotation of the pedals, she found that the sensation of motion was very familiar; and when it bounced over a stone and took off into the air she found it was very familiar indeed. She coaxed it back down to the road, only for it to take off once again from the crest of the hump-backed bridge. For all that it made the climb out of the valley considerably less tedious, Sarah was relieved that it was tea time and that few would therefore be watching the road. She was more relieved still to dismount with some degree of dignity and lean the bicycle up against the wall of the Crowthornes' cottage.

She rapped sharply at the door. It was a few minutes before anyone answered her knock. That was not surprising. The door opened slowly, cautiously. That was very surprising: usually labouring women and their worried husbands were only too glad to see her.

In fact, it was not Rosie Crowthorne who was peering around the edge of the door, but her sister Laura. "Mrs. Lovage!"

"You seem surprised."

"We weren't expecting you so soon."

"Well," said Sarah, "here I am, so why not let me in?"

As the door opened a little further, she could see Rosie standing at the foot of the staircase, looking somewhat startled but by no means in need of her assistance yet. There was no emergency here. What had got to Aggie?

"Come in, Mrs Lovage," Rosie said. "Please."

She crossed the threshold, automatically murmuring the words of protection as she did so. One might as well be on the safe side.

Rosie made a respectful little bob, the size of her belly making it awkward. "We weren't expecting you."

"Your sister said that. But Mrs. Banks asked me to look in on you, so here I am." She took two steps further inside.

Laura remembered herself. "Would you care for a cup of tea, Mrs. Lovage?"

"That would be very pleasant; thank you. And Rosie, you can sit down and tell me how you are."

They went to the kitchen. Laura fussed around with teapot and tea leaves. Sarah waited until the cups were full before she extracted from Rosie the details of her condition. There were cramps in the legs, pain in the back, heartburn and belching, but those were to be expected. Nothing seemed amiss at all. Sarah grew more and more puzzled. Was Aggie losing her touch? There would be nothing to be done for hours yet.

Having exhausted her reserve of questions, she suggested that Rosie might as well lie down for the time being.

Accompanied by the wide-eyed Laura, Sarah made a circuit of the little house, paying particular attention to the doors and windows, the chimney and the thresholds. Laura might prove to be more trouble than she was worth, if not carefully handled, and so Sarah made more of a show than she usually would have done. After all, the words would be just as efficacious if spoken out loud, and the fennel would do no harm, and smelled pleasant.

When she had finished, she remarked, casually, "You didn't seem keen to let me in."

Laura bit her lip. "Rosie had a letter," she said. "Her husband's on his way back. And you came before we had sent for you—well, for Mrs Banks—so we thought you might be him."

Crowthorne was a sailor, which was a mercy in that it kept him away at sea for months at a time, and a pity in that it encouraged his natural bent towards drink and violence. He had been away from Tilford for some time, and Sarah could not help but think it unfortunate that he should return now. His presence was not likely to make his wife's travails any easier.

"Do you know when he'll get here?"

Laura shook her head. "Any day. Any time."

Sarah frowned. "Come," she said. "Let's see how your sister fares."

Laura followed her up the stairs. Outside, the rain began to fall.

Rosie was in bed, but awake, curled on her side with her eyes wide open and a loose lock of hair falling across her face. She was unsettled, Sarah thought, and that was no way to go into a birth. The rain fell harder, spattering against the glass of the window.

Then they heard something else. The rattle of the doorknob. A curse. A knock.

The door was neither locked nor bolted, but Sarah had set her charms carefully. Anything that intended good to the expectant mother would be free to enter. Anyone who intended anything less, would not.

"It's him," Rosie breathed.

Now, he yelled. "Where's that slut who calls herself my wife?"

Drunk, Sarah thought, and dangerous. Now she knew why Aggie had sent her here early. Had they waited until they were sent for, they would have been too late.

She went to the window. Crowthorne was an unattractive sight, damp and hatless, with a bloodied right hand. Sarah opened the casement and called down, "Go away, please, Mr. Crowthorne. This is no place for a man."

He looked up, scowling. "Meddling old cow! Get out of my house!"

"I'm engaged by your wife, Mr. Crowthorne, and not by you."

"Why are you here, hag? Your usual business? The brat you catch won't be mine, if that's the way of it."

She did not know if that was true, and did not care. "That, Mr Crowthorne, is most definitely *not* my business."

He responded with a thunder of blows to the door. It held— it was bound to hold—but Sarah did not know how she was to convey that assurance to Rosie, who was pale and shivering with fright. She cursed under her breath. She had delivered babies under less propitious circumstances, but this was by no means ideal, particularly not for a first labour.

Laura joined her at the window, which seemed to infuriate Crowthorne still further. "You little tart! What are you doing in my house?"

"Can't I visit my own sister?"

Sarah was impressed by her defiance, though could have wished for a greater degree of discretion. She glanced behind her and saw Rosie's frightened face. It would do no good to continue matters up here. She shut the casement and clicked the latch into place. "Stay with your sister," she said to Laura. Then, closing the bedroom door behind her as she went, she marched downstairs.

She bent to peer through the keyhole.

He seemed to have the same idea. She smelt the spirits on his breath. His eye, cold and blue and malevolent, met hers. "I'll kill her," he promised. "And if I have to kill you to get to her, then I'll do that too."

"On the contrary, Mr. Crowthorne," she said. "You will not come in."

She took her handkerchief and stuffed it into the keyhole, muttering a charm against disturbances as she did so. Once completed, she straightened and stood back.

"Mrs. Lovage!" It was Laura's voice, shrill with alarm.

"On my way." She hurried back up, taking the stairs two at a time.

She found Rosie seated on the edge of the bed, leaning forward, with her elbows resting on her knees, and breathing heavily. Laura was mopping at a pool of liquid on the floor with a rag.

A quick glance reassured Sarah that all was as it should be. "You make yourself as comfortable as you can," she told Rosie, "and I shall be back as soon as I'm sure we'll have no further trouble from that husband of yours." She glared at Laura, willing her not to upset her sister.

She went back downstairs and peered out of the kitchen window. She could not see Crowthorne, but that meant nothing. He might well still be out there. And all she could do was go around all the doors and windows again to strengthen the wards.

When she was done, she listened, and heard only the patter of raindrops and the harsh call of a rook.

The rain began to fall a little more heavily, and Sarah reached out and drew the sound of it around the house like a curtain. Let it fall, drumming, thrumming, soothing; let it make a soft grey blanket, keeping those within safe from any harm that might come to them. . . .

Although she could not shake the picture of Crowthorne lurking just out of sight of the window, Sarah had a nasty suspicion that he had made off with Aggie's bicycle—which only went to show that he was as good as a stranger in Tilford, not to mention a fool. Well, she'd face Aggie later and confess. There were other things to think about now.

Once again she climbed the stairs to see to Rosie.

"Ah," she said, "we'll do nicely now."

That was true, truer than she'd feared it might be. Even so, it was a long night. The rain beat harder and harder against the roof and the windows; lightning split the sky across the valley; thunder broke into Rosie's gasps and groans. Laura, dozing in a chair, woke with a little scream, and Rosie sent her from the room with curses.

The storm passed over. The rain eased off and ceased entirely around dawn. Laura made tea and sugared it well; buttered bread and brought it upstairs. The day brightened, and Rosie, tired and sweating, submitted over and over to the relentless contraction and dilation of her own body.

There was no further trouble from the man Crowthorne.

༄ • ༄

It was a little while after noon that Rosie uttered a great roar, and grasped her sister's hands with a grip strong enough to bruise her. Sarah, on her knees behind Rosie, caught the bloody, slippery, squalling body, and passed the new child to the new mother. A few minutes more saw to the afterbirth.

It was only when Rosie had the tiny boy at her breast and Laura was once more wiping the floor that anybody thought to ask, "Where is he? My husband? Where did he go?"

"To the Royal Oak?" was Laura's suggestion.

Rosie sighed and glanced down at the tiny child. "It'll be worse when he comes back."

Sarah went around the house again and repeated the charms. It was not something that she would usually have troubled herself with, but one could not be too careful with a man like Crowthorne around. Then, having delivered herself of salutary advice and hints, she set off home.

The day was bright, the sunlight shining through the young green leaves and glinting in the puddles left by last night's storm. Sarah only remembered about Aggie's bicycle when she was half-way down the hill. She had left it in plain sight, and would have seen if it had still been there. Someone must have made off with it. More fool them. Anyone from 'round here knew that no good came of laying hands on things that didn't belong to them.

Aggie was up and dressed, sitting next to the kitchen fire with a cup of hot tea held in her hands. She tried to look angry, but it was by no means convincing to one who had known her as long as Sarah. "There you are. I was worried, when young Jimmy brought the bicycle back."

Sarah sat down at the table. "It's here?"

"Well, of course it is. You think any of the lads around here wouldn't know it for mine and bring it back here, even without the wards?"

"And undamaged?"

"I might get it some new grips for the handlebars. The leather's a little scorched. Other than that, no, there's nothing that won't wash off. I told you it works the same as a broomstick. No, I was worried about *you*, you silly baggage."

"There's no need," Sarah said, trying and failing to suppress a yawn.

"*Was* there trouble?"

"She did well enough, for a first time." She chuckled grimly. "The husband turned up. But he went away again."

"Ah," said Aggie. There was an odd note in her voice.

Sarah looked up. "What is it?"

"Jimmy told me. They found him. Caught on the weir down at Stoughton."

"Dead?"

"Dead."

Sarah nodded, slowly. "Well, I doubt there'll be many mourners. Rosie was scared of him. So was her sister." She paused. "Your bicycle. Works like a broomstick, you said?"

"That's right," said Aggie. "It does."

∽ • ∾

STOUGHTON GAZETTE, 24 March 1890

The death of VICTOR JAMES CROWTHORNE, able-seaman, of Old Mill Cottage, Tilford, was last Thursday inquired into by Mr. F. Dodd, coroner. The body of Mr. Crowthorne was discovered by Philip Heaney, bargeman, at six o'clock in the morning of Wednesday, 12 March.

Mrs. Rose Crowthorne, wife of deceased, identified her husband's body, and reported that he had returned to his home after a period of six months away at sea, at around seven o'clock in the evening of Tuesday, 12 March. She being at that time in an extremely delicate condition, he was dissuaded from entering the house. This was attested to by Mrs. Herbert, Mrs. Crowthorne's sister, and Mrs. Lovage, midwife.

Mr. Thos. Warren, of the Royal Oak, Tilford, testified that Crowthorne had been in the inn consuming ale and spirits until around half-past-six in the evening of 12 March, but that he had not seen him afterwards.

Dr. Harrison attributed death to drowning, but drew attention to curious marks, such as might have been caused by burning, across the palms of the deceased man's hands. The foreman of the jury, Mr. Nathaniel Fowler, reminded those present that the night in question had been notable for a severe thunderstorm, and suggested that the deceased "might have been resting his hands on the iron railing of Tilford Bridge at the moment when it was struck by lightning; which shock would also have been sufficient to send him into the river." Dr. Harrison agreed that this might have been possible.

The jury returned a verdict of accidental death.

LUNAR CYCLES

Gretchin Lair

New Moon

. . . The breeze flutters the edges of my cape as I walk through the meadow. I pick bright dandelions and the last of the wild roses, murmuring a blessing as I touch each one, grateful for the abundance. The new moon holds potential and possibility in her slender arms, so this is a time for preparation.

As soon as I post, the likes begin rolling in. I linger a moment, letting the fantasy fade, then close my laptop. I can hear the neighbors fighting next door, dogs barking down the hall. Outside, a motorcycle revs its engine even though it's stuck at a red light on my busy street.

I am a green witch trapped in a 300-square-foot apartment downtown. I write popular posts under the name Crow Moon about magic and Magick, pretending I gather herbs from forests and bathe in crystal lakes, creating potions and treats with mystical energies. Everything is carefully staged and crafted: the photo essays attract followers; the income from my video channel funds this tiny apartment; my online store pays for (most of) my meals.

Of course, you can be whoever you want online. You can be many different people. But I cannot be who I was, and I do not want to be who I have become.

A delivery truck rattles by. I splash my face with the last of the water I placed in the window to capture the light of the spring equinox. I braid my long hair on both sides. It's hot today. It's hot every day, caught in a canyon of concrete and wrapped within the spiral of climate change. I mist an air plant in a trapezoidal glass enclosure, a speaker's gift from the Coven-tion, an annual witch conference.

I step onto the sidewalk in the June heat and just barely miss being hit by a bicycle. "Hey!" I shout, and then touch the sodalite stone at my neck, telling myself to be calm and let be. The bicycle skids to a halt, the rider flashing a huge grin at me. "Hey!" she yells back, pink and bronze hair overflowing from a scuffed black helmet with stickers plastered over it. "Don't I know you?" She deftly hops off her bike and turns to face me.

"Blessed be," I murmur as an apology, turning and walking the other direction.

"No, wait!" she calls. "Crow Moon, right? I saw you at the Coven-tion! Oh my God!"

I feel her link her arm with mine and somehow we are walking together as naturally as if we are lovers, which is quite a trick because she's also guiding her bike by the handlebars, navigating it around sign posts and garbage cans and piles of who-knows-what. I am usually very conscious about boundaries, but this woman has such ease I let her do it. The sun is in Gemini. That must explain it

She keeps chattering, both charming and overwhelming me.

"I'm Crystal. You signed my book! Do you *live* here? I thought you must have been visiting! I thought you lived in the mountains somewhere!"

After a slightly awkward yet intriguing conversation, she looks at her watch, one of those fancy electronic ones. "Oh, no! I'm late for a date. You should come see me some time!"

She hands me a card for a bike shop named Raven Rides. As someone whose screen name borrows from corvids, the serendipity surprises me. But I haven't ridden a bike since I was a kid. Certainly not in these streets.

I offer a polite response and traditional fare-thee-well. She grins again, and I can see bright flecks in her dark eyes like stars reflecting in a deep lake. "See you later, Crow Moon!" She hops on her bike and is gone, her card in my hand like a dark, glossy feather.

Waxing Moon

. . . *The waxing moon is a time to take action. Today I am transplanting vegetables into the garden. The tomatoes sway on their sturdy stalks as I place them in the warm soil, leaving their fresh green aroma on my fingers. I will build trellises for the peas to climb. Everything we touch in this phase will be carried with the light of the moon throughout the month, so be sure to build with kindness and generosity.*

I carefully select a stone from the display and take it to the register. The shop owner doesn't seem to know I am Crow Moon, and I have never told her. She describes its qualities as she wraps it in tissue paper, even though I already know rose quartz facilitates unconditional love—towards oneself or others. I nod politely and escape as quickly as possible, emerging into the bright sunlight.

When I venture out, I often reward myself with ice cream. But on a day like today, my favorite ice cream place is packed. As I turn around to walk home, I catch my reflection in the window next door and stop suddenly when I see the sign for Raven Rides. I hesitate, but not for long, choosing to honor the pull of the waxing moon.

The woman at the counter is not Crystal, and I don't know whether to be relieved or disappointed. She barely glances at me as she spins a wheel on a bike hanging from a metal pole. I stand in the doorway, not sure whether to say something. When she remains silent, I look around the shop waiting for something to catch my eye so I don't look like I made a mistake by coming in.

All bikes look the same to me: thick frames and bold logos, built for people who are athletic. White, blue, red, black. This shop doesn't have air conditioning and I feel myself start to sweat. I've spent enough time pretending to look at these machines. Maybe I can make some strawberry basil ice cream when I get home.

Just as I turn to go, Crystal emerges from a curtained doorway. Her hair is more rose-gold than I remembered. She is wearing a torn T-shirt with the phases of the moon on it, accented with a silver Leo pendant and chunky amber earrings. I am dressed much more plainly, as I usually am unless I am speaking at an event.

"Hi! Can I help you?" she asks. I look to the woman at the counter, who continues to ignore us. But before I can say "Blessed be" and flee, Crystal recognizes me.

"Oh! It's you! Hi!" She hurries toward me, smiling widely. "I'm so glad you came!" I can't help but smile in return. "Are you interested in a bike?"

Oh, no. I'm definitely not. But I can't say that. "I was just at the crystal shop and passed by. . . ." I trail off, unsure where to go from there.

Crystal laughs, a sunny sound. "Oh, yeah! I keep meaning to go in there! Did you get anything?"

I pull the rose quartz from its slim paper bag and unwrap it. Crystal takes it from my hand. I am appalled at her lack of permission, delighted by her delight, and enchanted by the touch of her fingers as they skim my palm. I stare at the small ankh tattooed at the base of her thumb, my gaze flowing up her arm through a tangle of tattoos that vanish beneath her sleeve.

"It's beautiful! What does it mean?"

I tell her and we effortlessly begin a conversation about different crystal characteristics, which she says she knows very little about. When I speak about something I know, my voice gains confidence and clarity, and Crystal's eyes shine as she rubs the stone between her fingers.

Somehow we move from crystals to plants. I'm telling her about the medicinal properties of ferns when Crystal suddenly exclaims, "You know what? I just thought of something. Come here."

Still holding my quartz, she strides to a row of used bikes hidden from view when I arrived. Even I can tell these bikes are slightly different: older, slimmer, more relaxed and elegant. She unlocks a forest green one with a brown wicker basket.

"You've ridden a bike before?" she asks, clearly expecting the answer to be yes.

"Well, yes, but—"

"Great! I think this one would be perfect for you."

"I haven't ridden in a long—"

"Oh, that's OK! If you want to take a test ride, there's a bike path a few blocks away. It goes all the way to Lowell Butte—but that would be a very long test ride!"

I feel flustered, reaching for any excuse to end the conversation. "I can't really afford. . . ."

Crystal continues as if I hadn't spoken. "Oh! The Midnight Moon ride is coming up! You should come! I'd let you ride this bike."

It's too much. I can't answer. I hold out my hand. "Can I have my crystal back, please?"

Crystal blinks, then laughs. She returns the quartz, still warm from her hand. "Sorry! Sometimes I get too excited. Seriously, though. You want to go for a bike ride sometime? We'll take it slow." She pauses and says earnestly, "It's as close to magic as you can get. It's like flying without a broom."

This time she waits for an answer, and when I agree, she hugs me.

Full Moon

. . .*When the full moon rises, it frosts the fir branches with silver light, even though this is the heart of summer. I rise, lifting my hands to her as she shares her glow with me. Even in the stillness, there is sound. The soft call of the owl, the humming of the cicadas, and my own breath weave together into one song: may all be well, and all be well, and all manner of things be well.*

This has been the fullest moon in a very long time, overflowing with discovery and emotion. The moon is at perigee, so that makes sense.

Having a bicycle has changed everything for me. I'm so attached to it I'd call it a familiar, if such things were possible. I call her Fern. Crystal is right; she really is magic. I have a distaste for noisy, dirty machines, which is why I don't have a car or ride the bus. But Fern is as quiet as the wind in the forest, and like the wind, she takes me everywhere I want to go.

When Crystal takes me to Lowell Butte it feels like a dream. I wander for hours, occasionally stopping to gather plants I've only written about, like goldenrod, starflower, and nettles. I love seeing the striped caterpillars on ragwort that will become glorious cinnabar moths. We even see a deer in the old apple orchard at the top of the butte. She calmly watches us with dark eyes, then flicks her ears and slowly disappears into the tall grass. I barely believe I can come back whenever I want.

Not long after, Crystal cajoles me into joining her annual Midnight Moon ride. I astonish myself by participating with hundreds of others, most of whom are skyclad. I am too modest to be entirely nude, but the feel of the summer air on my skin beneath the stars (I can still see a few, even in the city) is exhilarating.

But I cannot write about these activities online. Online communities, even witches, are not very tolerant of deviation. I've been the target of a witch hunt before, and I don't want to be again.

So I feel stretched between all these different lives: the one I invent online, the one I am exploring with Fern and Crystal, and the one I wake to alone in my tiny apartment. I have been meditating with selenite to bring healing energy into my life, trying to open the channel to transformation and resolution. It's not working. When I ride Fern, though, I feel free and open, as close as I have ever felt to my true self. Or at least, the one I used to be.

OK, here's what I really can't write about:

Last night Crystal invites me over to her place. I'm nervous but excited. Being a witch, even a popular one, has been lonely. I feel confident online, but in person I'm shy. I can see the threads that connect everyone, but I am outside the web. Nobody wants what I have to offer in person—I'm too weird, or not weird enough.

Crystal is the first person in a long time who really seems to see me.

Crystal's apartment is stuffed with candles and plants and books and art. It's larger and much messier than mine. She places the lavender I've brought into a recycled bottle before introducing me to her black rabbit, Hecate, who is adorable and grumpy at the same time.

After pouring us some iced tea from a mason jar, Crystal flops on the couch. "Come here," she says. "I want to read your cards."

I kneel on the other side of the coffee table, but she smiles and pats the futon, which is covered in a dark woven blanket with the sun in its center.

"Sit next to me. I want to do this *with* you, not for you or *to* you. What deck do you want to use?"

She has over a dozen. I only have one. As Crow Moon, I prefer to live simply, never having more than I need. Tonight, I pick an elaborate deck with Art Nouveau illustrations.

When I sit next to Crystal, our legs are touching through my skirt. I feel my heart beat in my throat while Crystal asks what kind of layout she should do.

"Past, present, future?" I suggest timidly. Tarot has never been one of my strengths. I prefer astrology, because it's connected to the seasons and the earth in a way I find comforting, everything moving in celestial spheres with or without us. Unlike other witches, I seek guidance from the stars as they are, not as they were thousands of years ago. They've drifted over time, and I was genuinely shocked to learn most witches insist on using outdated divinations. I called it a "fiction" once. I paid dearly for that.

"OK, let's see what's in your past," Crystal says teasingly as she shuffles. She lays down the first card slowly, dramatically, flipping it over at the last moment to reveal The Moon.

"Ohhhhh!" she says. "Look at that! A *Crow* Moon!" She tilts her head to look at me, smiling. "Yeah, I can see it. Intuition, subconscious—well, you probably know this stuff better than I do."

"No," I say. "The cards don't speak to me. Is there more?"

"I hope so," she says, with the smallest of pauses. She turns back to look at the card: a woman in a white gown sitting with her knees drawn up, gazing at a crescent moon with gold foil stars glittering in a dark blue background. "The Moon is also about fear and illusion. Does that mean anything to you?"

Yes, I think, *that's true*. I am thinking of my whole life online, an illusion maintained through fear and inertia. But I don't want to agree too quickly, in case that will skew the rest of the reading, so I just shrug. "Maybe."

She blinks at me and her smile falters a little.

"You're not what I expected when I first met you," Crystal says, and I feel some part of me wilt. It's what I've always been afraid of, that someone will discover I'm not who I claim to be. My face, usually controlled, twitches.

"I mean, it's not bad," she says. "It's just interesting that I thought you were some mysterious, powerful figure and here I am reading your cards in my living room. I guess everyone is just normal when you get to know them." Her smile returns and I can feel myself breathe again.

She pulls a second card from the deck and lays it on the table. Two crystal goblets flank a winged lion's head.

"The present: oh, two of cups! That's a good card! I mean, I know there's not good or bad cards, but still!"

"Remind me what it means?" I ask.

"Yeah, it's a card for attraction, connection, love. . . ."

She turns toward me again and I flush lightly. "That's interesting," I say.

"Yes," she says, drawing the word out suggestively and raising an eyebrow, which makes her piercing catch the light. "Have you had any new lovers or unions lately?"

My flush deepens. "Um, no! Does Fern count?" *Do you count?* I want to ask.

Crystal laughs and takes the last card, my future card. When she flips it over, I frown. It's upside down, but I can see a man lying on the bank of a river with several swords thrust into in his back. Crystal frowns, too.

"But it's reversed," she says. "So it's not as bad as it looks."

"It looks pretty bad," I say, suddenly uncertain if we are looking at the past or the future.

We stare at it together in silence. The man is holding a rock in his hand, as if he tried to feebly defend himself before a mob attacked him. Crystal reaches for the deck booklet and says carefully, "OK, when it's reversed, it's more like hope, recovery, acceptance and renewal. We can work with that," she says.

"What's it mean when it's upright?" I say. I always want to know the worst-case scenario.

Crystal glances down at the booklet. "Betrayal, defeat, surrender, endings."

Just when I thought things were going well, I think.

Crystal sets the book down. "Don't worry about it," she says. "The cards aren't always right. And anyway, this means that you'll overcome it! Whatever it is. I'm sure you can whip up a counterspell. You're a great witch. You inspire so many people."

She looks at my face, my attention still on the card.

"You inspire me, at least," she says.

The world dims and slows as she reaches for me. When we kiss, she is as soft as an iris. The delicate bones of her face feel like china in my hands, her hair tangling in my fingers. I hear her gasp and my head swims. I had expected her to be the aggressor, yet find myself reaching and tasting, wanting more. I feel clumsy; I am afraid to scare her off, as if she were a rabbit or a doe. But then Crystal's eyelashes brush my cheek, delicate and electric, and I bury myself in the scent of rosewood, trying to remember everything, everything.

Waning Moon

. . . You've probably heard the rhyme "Horns to the East / Shine increased / Horns to the West / Moon take a rest." After shining so brightly for us, now the moon retreats in her eternal dance. This is her gift: to make room for darkness as well as light. Dance with her as you discover together what no longer serves you: illness, negative energy, emotions you want to heal and release.

"Lily!" It's been a long time since I've heard my given name. I am locking Fern to a bike rack, but I turn because I recognize Crystal's voice. I haven't heard from her since the tarot reading.

Crystal is waving as she walks toward me, her other hand entwined with the hand of a guy whose dark curls fall over his eyes. My stomach sinks. She introduces him as a "friend." I cannot remember his name or anything she chats about before they depart. He seems nice. She seems happy. I guess she always seems happy.

After that encounter, I stay away from the bike shop, letting Fern take me where she will. The pedaling soothes me. I discover a wetlands preserve where I collect wild ginger and watch muskrats float in the pond, their orange teeth glowing like embers in the water.

When I am home, though, I keep imagining Crystal skyclad with another, the image shifting between another witch, another woman, another man, another body. I know it's ridiculous. It's not like we were exclusive, or had anything more than that brief tryst. I light a candle in front of a mirror and say, "Any dark or evil thought may now return to its source." It doesn't help. I am tempted by darker magics: they say a witch who cannot hex cannot heal. But I cannot. I cannot. Might as well hex the moon for all the good it will do. I close my laptop, staring at the traffic lights as they turn from green to yellow to red.

I try to keep myself busy updating the sites I've neglected. I think I'm holding it together, until Fern gets a flat tire on the way back from taking photos on Lowell Butte. Everything is broken. I am heartbroken. I cry under the shade of a magnificent oak, rebuffing attempts from two cyclists who offer assistance.

Crying helps. I debate whether I should return to Raven Rides or seek another shop. But Raven is the closest. I need to learn to be brave and confront my fears for Fern's sake. She has become a steadfast and loyal companion.

Of course Crystal is at the counter today. Just my luck. I wrestle Fern past the door anyway.

"Lily! I haven't seen you around for a while!" I never should have told her my name. I wish she'd use my screen name.

"Crystal," I say formally, bowing my head slightly. I roll Fern toward her carefully. Crystal grabs the handlebars and pushes Fern to the silent woman, who unceremoniously but expertly lifts her into the bike stand. I wish they would take more care with her, treating Fern more like an injured patient than an appliance.

"A flat, huh? We'll get it fixed up. I guess this means you're keeping the bike?" She's wearing sacred geometry earrings that I can't help but see are shaped like daggers.

I nod.

Crystal tilts her head, fixing me with an intent stare. "OK, what's wrong?" I look at the woman at the bike stand, trying to decide whether to have this conversation now. She seems deeply focused on Fern.

"It's nothing," I say. "I was just wondering . . . about that guy you were with the other day."

"Emílio? Or Jason? Oh, right, you met Emílio. He's great. You two should hang out! He likes astronomy, too."

Astronomy and astrology are very different things. She should know that! I try to smile. "Thanks. I guess I'm just surprised I haven't heard from you lately."

"Well, I haven't had any questions about crystals or plants lately. But, yeah, we should totally hang out!" Crystal smiles, and I realize it will be up to me to make the next move. I need to learn to take more initiative. And yet I'm conflicted, because—are we just hanging out? Am I only a resource for questions she could learn by using a search engine or joining a witch community?

"Are you online?" I ask.

"Oh, hell no!" Crystal laughs. "Nobody is real online. I definitely prefer people in the flesh."

"Well, I mean, a community is what you make of it," I say, a little stiffly. "Regardless of where it is."

"I'm not big into 'communities,' either. Especially online. Too many people hide behind their keyboards. I'd much rather have a personal connection with someone."

"Well, what kind of witch are you?" I am startled to realize I don't know. "Because there are all kinds of...."

Crystal waves her hand. "Oh, I'm sort of an urban witch. I take a little of this, a little of that. I mean, I like learning stuff, but I don't really like labels."

I cringe despite myself. Crystal sees it, too. She says, "You have to make your own magic, Lily. Otherwise, what's the point of being a witch?"

I bite my tongue. I don't want to debate. I've never known how. I feel it in my bones: there is safety, security, structure in the Tradition. I know we can build more together than apart. And yet, the worst betrayal I have known was at the hands of my community.

I have always been a green witch, but I have not always been Crow Moon. I renamed myself after the thin, small moon that shivers in the bitter winds of February and March, when I was the target of a witch hunt. Before, I was known as StargazerLily, a young witch truly trying to understand the Path on which I wanted to walk. When I tried to make my own magic, I was branded a heretic. But Crow Moon is safe. Crow Moon always follows the rules.

Crow Moon is an imposter.

Crystal's words echo in me. *What's the point of being a witch?* As I fumble for a response, I feel her esteem for me plummet, and suddenly I am free falling. I watch the expressions on her face swiftly change, like a moon in time lapse, cycling from exasperation to scorn to dismissal. It's all happening so fast, as inexplicable and inexorable as a witch hunt. What's going on? How did we get here? I desperately wish I had a piece of blue lace agate to hold. It is a gentle stone, comforting in stressful situations.

When I don't know what to do, I just try to do the next right thing.

"How much do I owe you for the bike?" I almost say *for Fern,* but I don't want Crystal to know Fern's name, either.

She shrugs, her normally sparkling eyes dulled. "Eh. Take it. We're going to stop selling used bikes, anyway. Better to have the space."

Ah. Crystal cares no more for Fern than she does for me.

"I'd prefer to have no debts between us," I say.

Crystal frowns. "It's not a debt, Lily. God. Witches are so uptight sometimes." She looks at her watch. "Look, I have to go. Diane, can you take over for me?"

The woman working on Fern says, "Sure" without looking up. Crystal smiles her brightest smile, grabs her helmet, and says, "See you later, Lily!" A draft of rosewood reaches me as she passes and I am pierced by the memory of its scent before she is gone.

I wait for Diane to fix Fern's tire. I know she's heard everything. I awkwardly look at a rack of panniers and sadly finger a dying spider plant that's not getting enough light in this corner of the shop.

"It's ready." Diane shakes her head when I try to pay and silently hands me Fern. Holding her handlebars immediately brings me comfort. I'll be glad to leave this shop and take Fern where she belongs, into soft forests and wide meadows, without anybody else around.

As I reach the door, Diane says in a low voice, "It's not your fault, you know. Crystal never sticks to anything." I pause, suddenly realizing I am not the only one who has been hurt, or who will be hurt. Something catches in my chest; I think I will sob, but instead it's like thick clouds shifting to reveal a shining star on a November night.

"Thank you," I finally say, filling with relief and gratitude. I turn toward Diane, my hand on my heart as StargazerLily once would have done. "Blessed be."

Dark Moon

. . . The dark moon is a time for contemplation. The moon always reflects the light of the sun, but in this moment, the reflection must be internal. This is a time to review the past, develop insight, and acknowledge accomplishments. In this restful space, we honor the moon's whole journey before we turn, once more, toward the sun.

Witch hunts were once used against us, and now we use them against each other. Intimidation, shame and exclusion are useful, brutal tools. So I became what a witch is supposed to be. I was so successful because the expectations were so clear and so narrow; I never had to think about what I actually wanted. Ritual became routine became rote.

But looking like a witch doesn't make you a witch. It doesn't matter how many plants or crystals or cards you have. It doesn't matter how well you know the dance of the moon and the planets that waltz with her. It doesn't matter how many perfectly posed photos you post. How can we grow a community when we sow seeds of division? How can we grow anything in poisoned soil?

I am as slow to rise as the moon, but just as glorious when I am allowed to shine fully. It's time to plant my own seeds now, nurturing them even if I do not yet know what they will become.

My experience with Fern inspires me to create Lunar Cycles, an online "witches on wheels" group. "It's like flying without a broom!" I tell them. (Crystal grins and gives me a high five when I tell her that.) The group meets at Raven Rides every month: all kinds of different witches on all kinds of different bikes. It feels risky to create something unknown again. But when we ride together, bells ringing, lights flickering like stars, I am filled with such joy I think my heart will burst.

Crystal actually comes to our first event—which is good, because leading a ride is harder than I expect. She drops out after that, but I still see her at the shop occasionally. She keeps talking about leading a ride to draw a protection sigil on the streets using a GPS route planner. We'll see. I haven't read her chart yet, but Crystal must have been born during a new moon, brimming with energy that quickly wanes. That's OK. It takes all phases to make a complete lunar cycle. I am grateful for the fates that smiled briefly upon our crossroads.

I am equally grateful for Diane, who seamlessly provides quiet, steady support for us. Before our group rides, she offers to check all the bikes, airing tires and making minor adjustments before we leave. I always bring a little gift to express my appreciation: a bundle of herbs, dried flowers, stones, or bits of moss. I'm managing to coax her out of her shell a little: I can't believe *I'm* the talkative one! When Diane smiles, her gentle face blooms.

Tonight, on the last evening of the dark moon, I take Fern to look at my new community garden plot: a bare bed in a fertile landscape, waiting to be filled with whatever I can dream. It will be a place to grow what I cannot gather, a safe place for small seeds to sprout. Even though it is late in the season to start planting, I can begin with bulbs, cornflowers, snapdragons and sweet alyssum. They'll winter well, bringing color to the grey weather. Next year, maybe tomatoes and peas—everything I longed for and thought I could never have.

Tall sunflowers with heavy heads nod drowsily in the plot next to mine. Sitting on a little bench, the late golden light is hypnotic, filling me with a sense of ease which lingers even as the glow fades. The swifts and bats dart in the dusk. When the crickets begin singing their lullabies, I wheel Fern out of the garden and close the gate behind us. Tomorrow the new moon will rise, holding the old moon in her arms.

WORK ORDERS
∽ M.A. Blanchard ∾

Red ahead. Squeeze the brakes, left foot poised to shove off as soon as the lights change. Slept in again. Bike's headset makes an ominous creak every time I shift my weight. Hope I won't have too many work orders tonight, so I can fix it before handing the workshop over to the day shift. Tomorrow's my night off. Bike needs to be in tiptop shape for the moonlight ride.

Green. And go. Up and away, barely dodging an unsignaled right turn. Power down the long hill before the shop, so fast I'm almost in free-fall by the time I get to the bottom. That hill's the best part of my commute. Closest I get to flying, most days.

KJ's just closing up the storefront when I zip in the back. One minute late. Hang my bike from my hook—gotta love indoor employee parking—and help her take the signs down. "Busy day?" I ask, watching her count the till.

She nods, concentrating.

Looks like the shop'll make rent and pay off the distributors this month. Always a question with a small shop, especially one as weird as ours, so it's a relief every time we make it through.

I squeeze her shoulder in passing. "Come see me in the workshop when you're done. I'll get that brake rotor squeal out for ya."

Another nod. I head back into the workshop to get started changing the tires on Mrs. Jones's cargo bike. Shudder. What an awful job that'll be.

I work the late shift because the night riders all know my mom. Didn't inherit her aptitude for magic, but I'm a real wizard with a hex wrench. Around the time my parents were giving up hope I'd ever be witch enough to inherit the herb farm, Mom found out Aliane and Serena at Cimaruta Cycleworks wanted to expand their hours. She got me the interview, but my hands got me the job. Now I fix bikes after midnight and the night crowd keeps the shop afloat.

A lot of the night customers can't go outside during the day, so business boomed after Aliane started keeping the workshop open after dark. Take Mrs. Jones, for example, whose tire changes always make me want to go back to bed. Unspeakable, that design, the way it forces you to dismantle just about the whole back half of the bike to get the wheel off. But anyway. At night she doesn't look that out of the ordinary. Little pale. Nothing you'd look at twice. If you see her in daylight, on the other hand, it's obvious there's nothing alive inside that bloodless skin. Nice lady, though, and a good customer.

Ghouls don't bother me any, least not polite ones like Mrs. Jones. She wouldn't be caught dead doing anything so unmannerly as eating *living* people. Perish the thought. She's a great cook, too; her mixed-roadkill casserole is to die for. And so environmentally responsible.

Mrs. Jones depends on that cargo bike to deliver her meat pies, so it's a rush job. Just finishing up when she comes in.

"Oh my goodness, just look at her," she gushes, admiring the shine I'm putting on her rims. She'll tip me in homemade cookies regardless, but my favorite ghoul always gets a little more work than she asks for; she was kind to me during my most painful years as a failed teenage witch.

Tonight she delivers a big bag of oven-fresh yewberry and white chocolate chip. A deadly delicious combination. Immunity to plant-based poisons is the main thing I got from dear old mom and dad. Seeing as how she's already dead, poison isn't on Irma Jones's radar of things to worry about either. But speaking of things she does worry about.

"How's Maxie?"

She beams. We both know the light of her afterlife isn't destined to be my future husband, but she still hopes we'll change our minds. I definitely watched Max Jones eat too many voles when we were kids to ever want to lock lips. Nice ghoul, though, just like his mom.

"Top of his class! It's like he was born to be a mortician."

Like she's not even joking. Oh wait. She's not. Hard not to crack up imagining my childhood best friend all dressed up in a funeral suit. Wonder if he's ever tempted to snack on the bodies. Finger food for the hardworking funeral director. I'm awful. At least I manage not to laugh until his mom's out of earshot.

My mom drops by at midnight with lunch. I suppress the usual sigh when I see her gracefully alight outside the workshop door. Never quite got over wishing I'd at least inherited enough magic to fly. Broomsticks are kinda old-fashioned, but it used to feel so amazing when she'd take me for rides. Real downer when I got too big to perch on the back. It's not like there's a weight limit or anything; anyone can rock a broomstick if they're witch enough. I just didn't make the cut—the magic stopped recognizing me or something.

"Your favorite!" she announces, unwrapping an amanita-patterned cloth bundle on my workbench. "Frog paté on Irma's rye sourdough, with nightshade chutney and watercress."

Might be a failure as a witch, but at least my mom still loves me.

Cimaruta's not too far from my folks' place, so Mom comes by pretty often to eat lunch with me. She vanishes the grease off my hands with the merest twitch of her hemlock-stalk wand and pretends not to notice me stuffing sandwiches in my face as fast as politeness allows. Glad I've got Mrs. Jones's cookies to share for dessert.

"Are you doing anything fun tomorrow night?"

She worries I don't have a social life. I didn't for a long time, since the other teen witches ostracized me for not being able to fly. We've all grown up now, and most of them have long since apologized for the elitist enchantress phase, but Mom still feels bad about it.

"Going for a ride with KJ."

"Oh, how nice!"

Mom loves KJ. Our shop's evening part-timer has a nature thing going too, so she gets the parental stamp of approval. KJ's super modern about it, though, which I think is cool. After her geomancy apprenticeship, she went off to normie university to study earth sciences. Well-rounded perspectives are important, she told the coven. The real old-timers were shocked, but my parents said it was smart of her to be so open-minded. Mom hopes if I spend enough time with KJ some extra power might rub off on me. Don't think that's how it works, but what do I know about magic?

After Mom leaves, I dive into the night's final work order, swapping out the drivetrain on the local bridge troll's beloved fat bike. Geoff's another excellent customer. Never complains about the price, or the fact that we have to rebuild his ride several times a year. Mainstream bikes aren't built to take a rider who's eight feet tall and weighs half a ton. We keep trying to steer him toward a custom job from that welder witch with the cool hair, but he's too attached to trade up. We keep it going for him somehow; everyone here knows what it's like to love a bike beyond all reason.

Troll's bike's finally shifting good. Serena comes in to open up the storefront. Rats. Too late to do my headset now; day shift will need both workstands.

Creak my way uphill, wondering whether or not I should give in to the urge to have cookies for supper. Sun's rising. Shift up and pedal harder; I keep forgetting to stash sunscreen in my panniers, so I need to get home before I'm burned. Sleeping all day does nothing for my nonexistent tan.

$\wp \cdot \wp$

Mom drops by the apartment at moonrise to deliver a picnic for me and KJ. Not like I can't feed myself—or my friends—but it's nice of her anyway. She swapped out the frog paté for acorn and mushroom, since KJ doesn't eat animals. Still got some of Mrs. Jones's cookies left, thanks to the sense of duty that forced me to cook real food for both supper and breakfast. Guess we won't starve to death in the woods tonight.

I pack some extra tubes and chain links in my tool kit; fixing bikes is the one thing I do better than KJ, so I wanna be prepared for anything. Change my riding kit a couple of times just for something to do while I wait. Owl-print socks, or bats? Yeah, owls.

We ride out the old highway to the logging roads. The moon's so full we don't need lights. Headset's still creaking. Embarrassing. I'm so excited I can't stay focused on the shame, though.

KJ grins, moonlight flashing off her teeth. "Eager, much?"

Pause for a moment when we reach the end of the pavement. She smears the ointment over my frame. Her special blend of local clays pounded with psychotropic herbs from my mom's most fenced-in garden. Chanting, too quiet for me to understand. Probably not in any language I know anyway.

"Okay. Good to go."

Mount up. Moonlight lays a path along the logging road, silver and shadows forming the basis of our route.

KJ turns to catch my eye. "Ready?"

"Always."

She says something out loud. I still don't understand. Doesn't matter. She takes off in a shower of gravity-disrupted gravel, silver speedway waiting for her to start pedaling. The patter echoes as gravel rains off my tires and my bike follows hers into the air.

We don't do this often. Takes a lot of power for KJ to keep me in the air. She mostly rides the moon's path for her other part-time job, not just for the sheer joy of it. Witches wind up with work orders too. They just spend less time turning wrenches and more time tweaking hexes. I get to ride along a few times a year, when the magic's running high and she can spare the juice to float me a few feet above the ground. She's a good friend. These precious nights, I get to feel for just a little while like I'm the way I was supposed to be.

Fly in silence, following the logging road's twists and turns, pedaling on top of a moonbeam, almost like proper witches. KJ could use a broomstick if she wanted to. She goes out in daylight sometimes, though, when flying a broom might be a little conspicuous. Enchanted bikes look like regular bikes unless you have a certain sort of trained eye, so her ride's more multipurpose than a broom. And, let's face it, brooms are kind of dorky.

"So," KJ says after a while, "I don't suppose you brought cookies."

She's full of it. I always bring cookies. She told me once they were her favorite food. That was when I learned how to bake. Mrs. Jones's are better than mine, though, so I'm glad I didn't eat them for breakfast. Quick snack stop when the moon's path leads us over top of a massive boulder overlooking a night-filled abyss.

"You seriously have to get the recipe for these," KJ says around a mouth full of crumbs.

"I keep asking, but Mrs. Jones won't give it to me unless I ask her son out on a date."

Howl with laughter. Not that Max Jones didn't actually grow up to be pretty good-looking—he's just always so *clean*. Total yuppie. Feel like I'd have to get my mom to magic the grease off my hands any time I wanted to hold his. Awkward. Anyway, he doesn't even own a bike, so I don't know what we'd do for fun.

Hopped up on sugar and hilarity, we forget to fly quietly. A family of owls joins us for a while, hooting along with our laughter. Seems like they're having a good night too. Maybe they like my socks.

"I've just got one little job," KJ admits. "But don't worry, it won't take much. I'll have plenty of juice left to fly you home."

Land in a clearing, torn up where mountain bikers squished through in mud season. Looks like the scars of wounds that don't know how to heal all the way.

"This won't take long."

She waves me to a flat rock, out of the way. Unpack the lunch Mom packed for us, watching sidelong. Don't want her to think I'm staring.

She crouches by the tracks, hands in the broken dirt, muttering in that language I don't understand. Dirt moves. Compacted soil loosens, roots twisting out from the nearby grass to stitch the wounds together. KJ shifts her hands out of the way and lets the planet work, channeling just a little of her energy into the ground to jump-start the healing process. A shimmer of something in the air, warm and reassuring. In moments the tracks are gone, the clearing restored to the state it was in before anyone rode over it. Can't feel it myself, but KJ says that the wounded places, ones that have been disturbed in a way they can't refocus their energy around, disrupt the flow of the ley lines. It's how the geomancers find them and let each other know that there's work to be done.

"Mm, sandwich!" she says, joining me on the picnic boulder.

She's always starved after feeding her energy to the ground. Good thing Mom packed extra.

Wash it all down with a nice draft of hemlock-and-henbane punch. Mmm, poison.

KJ takes us higher on the way back, less concerned about conserving magic now that her single work order's fulfilled. We're nearing the treetops. Wait. KJ's fallen behind. Weird.

"You okay?"

She shakes her head. "There's something—" She points into the trees, off to one side of the logging road.

"Something bad?"

She nods. "I have to get closer. Do you mind?"

"Should we call someone?"

"No, it's fine. I'm sure I can handle it."

Steer our bikes off the road, zipping between trees. Have to be careful now, since my bike's not enchanted. KJ's has enough power in it to avoid obstacles on its own, but mine's just borrowing magic. Takes full concentration to avoid dinging an unsuspecting maple, so I don't realize we're there until the bikes drop groundward.

"Shhhhh."

Don't need her to tell me. Even I know something's not right here. Energy flow's been messed up. Bad. KJ looks sick.

We're at the edge of a big clearing. Big, and weird. Power leaking all over the place. Not used to feeling that much of it. No wonder she's nauseated. If the leaky magic wouldn't make it obvious enough this place has something major going on, the colossal oak in the center of the clearing is a dead giveaway. It rises up above the surrounding forest, standing guard over the land. The visible parts of its roots trace a winding path toward a spring. Moonlight shines off the dark water, illuminating the ripples. Powerful urge to take a drink, to quench the sudden dryness in my throat with the chill of blessed water. All around the oak, smaller plant life lies in broken ruins, brown and dying where it's been crushed at its roots. The entire clearing is cut up and dug into—heaps of earth mounded by the repeated passage of joyriders on ATVs.

"How could they?" she whispers.

Kind of glad I don't have an answer to that. Catch her bike as she propels herself off the saddle and darts forward to fall on her knees in front of the oak. Lean our rides by a fallen fir and follow.

The ground feels wrong. Something's missing, something important. Overwhelming sense of devastation. The oak's roots are all scratched up where off-road tires ground over them.

"You're going to have to help me," KJ says. "I can't do this much on my own."

Don't know what I have to offer, but I can't argue with her urgency.

"Just tell me what to do."

She settles among the damaged roots, leaning back against the trunk of the ancient oak. Never seen anyone look more like they belonged exactly where they were.

"I need water from the spring. And I need to borrow your energy."

"You know my energy's not good for much."

"It'll be enough."

She doesn't say *it has to be*. I know.

Empty our water bottles around the roots of some of the less-broken shrubs. Maybe it'll help them grow back. Fill the bottles from the spring and bring them over. She holds them for a moment, chants, gives them back.

"Sprinkle some of that around every plant in this clearing that's larger than a blade of grass."

Walk the outer perimeter of the clearing, widdershins. Squirt a few drops of enchanted water onto each and every plant. Bottles are empty. Refill. KJ lays her hands across the wet plastic, on top of mine. Something flows out of me, into her. For the barest fraction of a second I feel something bigger, beyond me, beyond her, beyond *us*. And it's gone. Back to watering widdershins, listening to KJ chant.

Hours pass. Something's moving, underfoot. Lose count of how many bottles of sacred water I squirt out, walking ever-smaller anticlockwise circles. KJ's voice has gone hoarse, but she's still chanting, pouring herself and whatever she got from me into the ground.

"Come up here," she says at last.

Look down. Realize I've watered the final jagged shrub. Standing right where the spreading roots converge. Walk, lightly as I can, over the tops of the roots. Press myself against the bark in imitation of KJ. She takes my hand and falls silent.

Don't realize anything's happening until it's almost over. Moonlight's long gone, replaced by the dark of night, then slow, creeping gray dawn. Blink once. Twice. Fell asleep for a while, standing. Back sore from leaning into the oak. The clearing's almost unrecognizable, heaped soil flattened down, gaping ruts healed over. Grass and shrubs knit together across the disturbed soil, weaving and winding, until the ground is whole.

Long slog back to the logging road. KJ keeps apologizing to the ground, wherever we can't help disturbing it.

"I'll come back later and fix you," she promises. "Right now I've got nothing left."

Eventually, we make it. Out of the thick forest, onto a surface already altered by humanity's repeated passage.

"You okay to ride?"

Not sure what I'll do if she says no. She grins.

"I'm always good to ride."

Mount up. Pedal. The moon's path is long gone. Without it there's no way for even a powerhouse like KJ to lift my regular old bicycle off the ground. Her bike can fly even when her magic batteries are fully discharged, but she stays down on the dirt and gravel with me.

"Sorry you didn't get your full quota of flying," she says. "I'll take you out again soon."

"Don't be sorry," I tell her. "You had something important to do."

"You helped, you know."

Still not sure what it was she took out of me. But it was something, and I know it made a difference. Never knew there was anything important inside my magic-deficient body.

"I don't mind if you fly home," I say. "You must be exhausted."

She shakes her head. "Can't. Had to drain the enchantment off the bike, too. Filling in those ruts took everything."

Weird to see another witch stuck on the ground. Ride for hours, mostly not saying anything. If not for my annoying headset creak, I'm not sure we'd stay awake. Guess in a way it's good I didn't get around to fixing it.

Eventually, we make it back into town. She's too tired to protest me riding a little out of my way to see she gets home in one piece. She looks like a plant that hasn't been watered enough, limp and empty.

"Get some sleep. Get *lots* of sleep. Call me if you need anything."

She laughs. "I'll be too busy sleeping to call. I'm just glad I don't have to work tonight."

Groan. Ah, right. Work.

I sleep like a log. Or maybe like a tree, since the sleep goes a long way toward healing me from the night's adventures.

∽ • ∾

Coast down the hill toward the shop. Too wiped out to race against my own best time today. Hope the work orders are light.

Building up a racer for one of the fae. Carbon fiber everything. Personally, I'm a believer in the doctrine of "Steel is Real". Guess when you're allergic to cold iron, though, carbon is a lot easier to tolerate. Looking forward to taking this one for a test ride when it's done. It'll be a real flying machine, even though it's not built for enchantment. Some bikes are just that fast.

"I brought you lunch again," my mom says from the doorway.

Didn't even see her land.

"KJ told me you were both up all night," she says. "She came by for a healing draught. I've never seen a witch so drained of magic."

Eat the sandwiches she brought me—frog again, my favorite— and think about how the grass and tree roots reached toward each other through the broken soil. How KJ's hand reached for mine the same way, like we had something to share.

"Something happened," I say. "I don't know how to explain it. There was something in me and it went into the ground, through KJ. I felt the earth. I felt *everything*. Just for a second."

She smiles.

"There isn't anyone who doesn't have at least a little magic in them," she says. "You just had the misfortune of growing up surrounded by people who wear theirs on the outside."

"So I didn't imagine it?"

"Of course not. I doubt KJ could have managed that without you there to draw on. It sounds like a job that really called for a whole coven. Your friend is very powerful, but still."

"If you could have seen it, Mom—there wasn't time to call for anyone. I think the clearing was dying."

She hugs me. "You did the right thing. Both of you."

Sigh.

"I wish I had more magic. I could have done more."

"Magic isn't everything," she starts, catching my eye. "Look at that bike. Those fae might be built for speed, but they can't even touch a bicycle until you've tucked all the cables inside so they won't get burned. They need a human who can touch tools, or else they can't race."

"I know, but—"

Stop. I've spent my whole life wishing I had more magic, but wishing never changed anything. Even in our world, wishing's just an old story. Making things happen takes hard work. Magic or not. I might not be much good with magic, but I've never had any problem with work.

"I'll let you get back to it," Mom says, seemingly reading my mind.

"Thanks for lunch. Again."

She flies away into the night sky, black robes rippling in the air currents. It's beautiful to see.

Finish the faery racer. Take it for a spin, pushing myself, pushing the bike, making sure the build is solid. Shifts like a dream. Push, like I'm racing the fae. Up, up, up to the top of the hill. And down. The flat aero frame is heavy, and I descend so fast I think for a second that the wheels have lifted off the pavement.

SUNBEAMS, IN THE FOREST
ᔆ Ether Nepenthe and Mohini Hirve ᔆ

The wheels of Vox's bike shrieked on the pavement as he plunged into the back alley. He flattened himself—and the bike—against the half-torn posters on the brick wall and held his breath. A whiff from a leaking gas pipe above blew down his neck, biting at the exposed stripe of flesh between his collar and his helmet. Rookie mistake; he should have tightened his scarf better than this. For now—

Boots stomped down Main Street.

Vox closed his eyes. A faint prickle of magic rose from the handle of his bike.

The footsteps grew louder. Drones spilled into the back alley, scanning for lifeforms.

Vox held his breath and focused on the tiniest flame of arcana twinkling a faint red in the limbo of his mind.

Outside, the pigs were running by, shouting and stomping, surveillance drones beeping and throbbing. The world was *loud*. Loud enough to cover the creaking of rubber against his skin, the drums beating under his skull, the baton he could almost hear smashing down his nose already.

But Vox held strong. In his mind's eye, he kept the dwindling, ethereal embers burning within the shelter of his gloved hands. He knew better than to fuel it back to blazing glory with his own will, but for now, just for now, it had to work.

The surveillance drones buzzed their way back to Main Street; the shouting and the stomping slowly faded away.

Vox opened his eyes and sagged on the handlebars, out of breath, with an ache in his jaw, in his legs, everywhere. His head was light and dizzy. He needed a shower and some binder-free time, like, yesterday, or maybe even two days ago. Time had become a blur, the battlestreets shadowed in a perpetual twilight. On top of it all, his voice modulator was glitching, which was hilarious for a guy who had called himself *Vox*, 'voice'.

Now, though, was not the time to worry about that. He swallowed back his rising panic and willed himself into deep, slow breaths.

He forced himself to continue as he stepped away from the wall, stretched his arms, and checked first his bike, then his surroundings. The rune on the handlebar was all but a faded mark now. It was barely visible under the flickering red light, which bathed the back alley and its uneven rows of pipes, broken windows, and piles of trash.

Vox continued to breathe slowly and deeply, his eyes scanning the wall until he caught the sigil he'd been looking for. A bunch of angular lines had been hastily drawn on a wooden plank barring down an iron door. Wood, huh? That, too, he should have known.

With one last bigger-than-necessary inhale, Vox crossed the alley, pulling his bike along. The closed-off door stood between a gaping rubbish bin and the orange-red corpse of a squirrel, slowly gnawed away by the same toxic gas that prickled Vox's neck.

Vox raised a tentative finger and traced along the sigil.

Nothing.

He dusted off his gloved hand on his thigh and tried again.

Still nothing.

Screams pierced through his helmet as he tried a third time, to no avail. They came from his right—from Main Street, where the pigs would still be roaming about. Looking for him.

Well. The rune wouldn't protect him a second time, not in its current state.

He tried a fourth time, muttering half an expletive, half a plea under his breath. This time, he pushed his finger so deep into the wood that a splinter pierced through his glove. He grunted and stepped back; a pale arm reached out, through the wooden plank and the iron door, ethereal and swift, and caught his wrist.

A yelp escaped Vox's lips. Drones blared at the entrance of the back alley. Flashlights blinded him, but he could not free his hand, and he sure as hell wasn't going to let go of his bike. He focused on the magic gateway opening before him. If he squinted hard enough, he could make out a pair of droopy, brown eyes.

"Please," he shouted, "the stars—they aren't really shining on my path right now!"

There was a loud, distinct tsk. "That's not even *close* to the password," said a voice with a thick southern accent.

"Sorry, I—"

Plump fingers let go of Vox's wrist and glided down the sleeve of his armored jacket to entwine with his. Drones and boots were running down the alley, shields shining in the neon light, acid mud splashing about. Gloved hands, tasers, batons, and—

Arcana surged all around Vox. He tightened his grip on both the hand and his bike. For one shining moment, the world was nothing but magic: no gravity, no need to breathe, no tether between his body and his soul.

Then, just as suddenly, reality settled down.

Vox's legs gave way under him and he held onto his bike, panting.

To think people *paid* to feel like *this*.

A green alert box flashed at the very corner of his visor, reading good air quality, a strange glitch over the owner's name, and "(they/them)". Vox took his helmet off, breathing in the heavy, musky smell of incense and burnt herbs as he unclenched his jaw and scratched his scalp. His hair was not liking all the helmet time it had gotten recently, but nobody remembered the air quality index ever being low enough to let them go outside bare-headed. He took his gloves off, wincing as he extracted the splinter from his finger, and scratched the space between his braids.

"You got the sigil wrong," a voice said somewhere to his left. "As in, right sigil, wrong way to trace it. Wrong order of the strokes. You're lucky I was keeping an eye on things."

Vox said nothing, stuck between "thank you for saving me" and "what do you mean, there's a right and a wrong way to do it?". Too much time had passed to answer, at any rate.

He wasn't sure how one went about making small talk to a witch, anyway. Maybe it didn't matter much. Maybe what mattered was that he wasn't in the back alley anymore. Even if he wasn't sure where he was, not exactly.

Well, at least he knew that he was in one of the messiest, most poorly-lit rooms he'd ever stepped foot in. One of Vox's roommates had untreated ADHD; he knew about messes. But this was something else entirely. Heaps of unidentifiable organic matter grew along the walls, which were lined with jars, books, papers, and plastic containers of various sizes. Tangled fairy-lights strung across the overflowing cabinets and seafire trapped in fishbowls at the four corners of the room lit the disarray in a glimmering, green-blue hue.

The only defined shapes Vox's eyes could make out through the overwhelming clutter were a large, mostly-organized desk against a wide window, and the witch who leaned against it. In the low light, their skin shone a pale, sickly gray, their painted lips the shade of the sun sheathed in clouds.

They cleared their throat and Vox startled, realizing he'd been staring at them absently.

"So," the witch said, cocking an eyebrow. "How may I be of service?"

Vox awkwardly patted the handle. "Need a good luck charm," he explained, forcing every single sound through icy walls of anxiety. "An invisibility charm? Uh. Uh . . . Blessing of . . . Daylight?"

"Blessing of *Dagaz*," the witch corrected. They tilted their head. "But Dagaz won't grant you invisibility. Quite the opposite, actually. *If* runes granted anything, which . . . they . . . don't."

"It's what I had before," Vox mumbled. He tapped the faded marking on the grip; it glimmered briefly with a faint red that echoed Vox's now well-chipped nail polish.

The witch hummed and pulled themself away from their desk to crouch down and observe the carving, giving Vox the opportunity to observe them more closely.

The witch was wearing combat boots, the vintage kind; loose dark trousers that gathered at the ankles; and a long, black, sleeveless jacket over a smoke-patterned sports bra in deep, shimmering red. No tattoos or bodymods in sight; not even earrings. A wreath of olive branches, with blooming lavender and other blue flowers Vox didn't recognize, crowned an uneven buzz cut. A sharp-looking dagger rested on their chest, like a necklace of sorts, right where Vox was pretty sure his stare would be unwelcome.

Vox pointedly directed his eyes elsewhere. The singular window looked onto a swirling sort of darkness, indistinct shapes and shadowy figures in shades of black and silver.

"Oh, you're far from the city now, kid," the witch said without looking up. "Private dome and all that. Wish I could afford to own it, though."

Vox nodded. A stone weighed on his chest, heavy and constrictive; a sour aftertaste dried his mouth. He took to fiddling with the straps of his gas mask to try and ease his ever-growing nervousness, idly noticing that his dark skin was tinged blue in the murky light of the room. The bright reds and yellows of his shirt and trousers had become muted purples and greens, all part of the same limited palette, no matter the base color—this was a witch's den, after all.

Silence slowly unfurled in the workshop. Long fingers of blue-silver-purple magical quiet reached out and muffled the various sources of noise—a buzzing fan here, a bubbling fishbowl, the window left ajar. Soon enough, all Vox could hear was his own heart, quickly beating against his rib cage. Even creasing the hem of his clothes or poking at the protective scales on his sleeve didn't make any sound.

The witch was now sitting in front of the bike, the lower half of their face in their hand, gently rocking back and forth. A lazy finger endlessly traced over the old rune as time stretched thinner in cold-colored stillness. No sound, and, now, no smell either. Not one draft of air, not one sensation; nothing but magic, filling up the room. Nothing but magic, seeping into the empty mason jars left open on the leaning shelves; the abandoned tea cups on the desk, the workbench, the sundries tray by the door; the space between Vox's fingers, his nose, his mouth—

"Alright," the witch said at the same time Vox started coughing out blue-silver-purple puffs of arcana. "Oi! Don't die on me."

"S-sorry," Vox stammered, hitting his chest with his fist. The witch's magic tasted metallic and cold, very bitter; it reminded him of that very expensive coffee they sold by the gram downtown— with a very surprisingly sweet aftertaste, round and soft.

The witch tsked and got back to their feet. "So, what do you need to be invisible for, anyway? I'm not sure I can tweak Dagaz like Madame Lou did. That's eir work, right?"

Vox nodded. "Well, I—"

"It's less invisibility and more like reflection," the witch explained, oblivious to the interruption.

Vox snapped his mouth shut. The witch limped over to their desk, reached out to switch a kettle on, the bright blue flame a beacon in the ambient arcana, and rummaged through an impressive collection of color-coded tea tins.

"Sure. My understanding is, you can't hide me from the—you can't hide me, but you can make it look—make me look, like . . . casual. Like I fit right in. Anywhere, any time.

The witch pursed their mouth, measuring a heap of tea leaves into a strainer. Vox gnawed his lip, not sure why he needed them to know that he understood the arcana.

He persevered anyway. "The way Madame Lou put it to me— you know that saying, if you want to hide, hide in the eyes of the sun? That's the basic idea, I think. The way the sun casts sunbeams on the forest floor—they'll think of me as just another sunbeam among many."

The witch scoffed. "You ever seen sunbeams in a forest?"

Cups clinked as they placed them on a tray. A pleasant smell rose, spicy and warm, and probably way too sweet—but not sweet enough for Vox to forget that gibe.

"I have. Online, I have. In VR, even," he protested.

"Of course." The witch smiled. "Sorry."

The apology sounded genuine enough. Vox took the cup that was offered to him. Golden-brown liquid swirled in the dark blue china; it spiraled and shone, unbothered, unchanged by the lights bathing the workshop. It really all smelled very sweet.

Magic tea, huh? Well, that was new.

"It's Comfort in a Cup," the witch said, absentmindedly motioning for a tiny drone-cart to come over, loaded with tools, herbs, mason jars, incense sticks, coal sticks, and several tarot decks. "You'd better make yourself at home, this might take a while."

Vox nodded, put the cup down on a plain surface, and took off his heavy-duty jacket. The reflective patches twinkled like a faulty neon sign; there was no chair to leave it on, so he folded it next to his helmet instead. The cup felt warm around his bare fingers; it was a pleasant, reassuring warmth. The room itself felt pleasantly, reassuringly warm, for all its blue-purple-silver hue and no fresh air.

Vox stretched and brought his attention back to the cup. He had no desire to chat with the witch, but neither did he wish to drink magic beverages so trustingly.

"What's it do?" he asked.

"Hmm?"

"The tea. What does it do?"

The witch stopped mid-way into spreading their implements on a star-patterned towel. "It's called 'Comfort in a Cup,'" they said, very slowly. "It's—I mean—" They groaned and put their tools down. "Sorry." They closed their eyes and sighed. "Sorry—yes, you have anxiety and I'm being snarky. Not helpful." They raised a hand in appeasement. "It's been a day. I mean, a week. A month. A year. A life."

Vox nodded. He could relate to that.

"Anyway." They sighed again. "It should—it's what it says on the tin, really—should taste like comfort, safety, relaxation. It will not replace therapy and it will not, uh, trip you up or anything, but it'll help you not cPTSD all over the place."

Vox blinked. "How. . . How do you know I have. . . .?"

The witch shrugged. This time, they didn't even look up. "You're a trans kid of color living in this wretched hellscape of a world—possibly neurodivergent now that I'm thinking about it—*of course* you've got cPTSD. If not PTSD, period. I mean. You've got a militia-grade mask, and you're riding a bike that's seen action on the streets." They ran a finger along the top tube. "The frame—tsk. I don't like this saying, but it's true: just like your body, the frame of your bike remembers." They rubbed their thumb against their index finger. "Also, you didn't do a very good job of cleaning off that blue dye from the water cannons."

Vox hummed. At this point, he had gathered that the witch was definitely rude, but that they were trying not to be, in their own way. Or maybe he was still avoiding conflict, because pigs were easier to deal with than telling some weird stranger who could pull magic portals out of back alleys that what they'd just said wasn't very cool, and could they please not over-analyze him like that? Easier to address any prevailing crisis at hand than to confront the discomfort thrumming through him.

With another tsk, the witch waved the cart-drone away. They reached out their right hand and breathed out. Vox was trying not to stare, but he knew the whirring of a bionic limb expanding when he heard one. Right now did not seem like a good time to comment out loud how he'd heard most witches stayed organic, what with the sparks flying and the arcana surging as the witch's silver fingers blurred and etched into the metal.

Eventually, his mistrust of the tea surrendered before the dreadful prospect of discussing his feelings, and he took a sip.

It tasted as sweet and warm as it smelled, even though Vox couldn't tell what it tasted like exactly. Memories flashed before his eyes: coffee on a rooftop at five AM, after a really good party; braiding his roommate's hair, chit-chatting on an endless summer afternoon; rolling around in his winter duvet, heavy and cozy-warm.

Maybe he knew comfort, but he didn't know safety. The thought would have been sour in any circumstances, but now, as he licked golden glitter off his lips, it was only bittersweet.

Vox took another sip.

The shop was quiet, full of white noise buzzing along with its owner's humming. Vox's shoulders relaxed first, then his neck, his legs, his ankles. He leaned against a set of mismatched shelves and, three sips in, realized he could breathe much better than he had in a long time. His ribcage was extending, like the tide rolling onto an amber shore.

The place didn't seem so dark, now that his eyes had gotten used to it. Vox could even tell there was some order to the chaos surrounding him—those were clearly local, mediterranean herbs, while this pile only dealt with stuff from abroad. Idly, he wondered if the witch had a garden of their own somewhere under that private dome they had mentioned. Vox had seen gardens before, but only in VR.

"Have *you*?" he asked after a while, and his voice sounded deeper and mellower to his ears, calm and grounded.

"Have I what?"

"Seen them. Sunbeams. Have you ever seen sunbeams in a forest?"

The witch stretched with a groan, and their fingers slotted back into place, the silver glimmering as it regained the color of their skin. They sighed loudly and reached out for their cup, taking a sip of their much darker brew before answering.

"It's not as magical or dreamy as you might think. It's just . . . light. Shadows. It's nice. Soft on the skin—you can't feel it, but you can see it, and it looks so soft on the skin." They stretched their neck and looked at him, pensive. "You know, thinking back on it now . . . I could feel this"—they gestured around at the arcana—"so much more strongly then. It's been harder since, even though the enchantments, the magic, is everywhere—even here, even now. But I wish I had known to look more closely, to remember the feeling of being immersed in it all."

They shook their head and returned to their work.

Vox swallowed down the melancholy lurking under the honey-sweet taste of the soothing tea. Was that all there was to hope for—sadness, under the illusion of comfort? A lull in the struggle, in the fight, a hint of incense instead of a cloud of tear gas?

And yet.

Even if this was all there was—he refused to believe so, but even then—Vox would still keep moving. He would still hop on his bike, deliver messages and supplies, rescue pets and children alike. What else was there to do but fight when you could and try to care for yourself in the interim?

Vox took another sip. He'd take the illusion of comfort over the awareness of the lack of the real thing, any day. Gold swirled up and the cup refilled. *Neat.*

The cup never emptied until the witch got back on their feet with a grunt, and Vox knew they were done.

"There you go," they said, tapping the handle. The rune shone a fierce red, along with several others, which now marked the grips, the pedals, and the stays. "I'd explain what they do, but I can't give away my trade secrets, now, can I?"

They were smiling, but sweat beaded on their temples and they were leaning against the edge of their desk for support.

"I can only pay for one of these," Vox admitted, sheepishly putting the cup back onto the tray.

"Pay?" The witch cocked an eyebrow. "Kid, I don't do paying."

"Don't call me that," Vox said, talking too fast for his anxiety to shut him up. "I really don't like it when people call me that."

The witch raised both hands. "Got it. Sorry."

"Thanks."

"Mh."

Silence. The witch busied themself with the tray. Vox fiddled with his gloves, slowly putting them back on.

"You don't do paying," he said slowly, unfolding his jacket. "but I still owe you, right?"

The witch looked at him wordlessly from behind a tankard-sized tea mug.

"I could do a gig or two for you—"

"Easier than that." They dried their mouth with the back of their hand, their lipstick somehow unsmudged. "For today's work, all I need from you is for you to stay alive and be well."

Vox tilted his head. "What?"

"That's my demand—the favor I'm asking of you. Stay alive and be well. Don't go and get yourself killed or caught or anything. Stay alive and well."

That was ridiculous. That was the most ridiculous thing he'd ever heard. Witches were always like that. You expected them to go, 'bring me the head of the police union leader' or 'fill my bathtub with transphobic tears', and then they pulled stuff like this. Vox gave a weak, awkward chuckle, because what else could he do? They seemed really serious about it, too.

"Okay. Thanks. I-I'll do just that. Uh. I'll be on my way now. This—this brings me where I came from, right?" he asked, pointing at the door behind him.

The witch motioned for him to go on. Vox put his helmet back on and pushed the bike along. He had barely reached out for the door handle when the witch called for him.

"You should come back soon," they said, arms crossed on their chest. "If you want more tea and stuff. Also, sometimes I do need a courier. We could work something out."

Vox smiled under his helmet, tiny smileys transcribing the expression on his visor. "Thanks. When the streets don't need me anymore, I'll think about it."

The witch tsked. "The streets will always need you," Vox heard them shout as he stepped into the void. "The work's never done! Don't overdo it or you'll end up like m—"

The door closed behind him like a thud. Just like on the way in, magic surged, the sensors in his helmet went haywire, and then

Vox was back in the same alley. A very bleak, pastel dawn was rising over a city that never slept, and he had work to do.

As he settled onto the saddle, Vox realized he had forgotten to ask the witch their name—or what the correct password was.

Maybe that didn't matter much.

Maybe he'd ask when he came back.

WHEN MASTERED, A GRACEFUL ACCOMPLISHMENT
∽ *A.P. Howell* ∾

"No library for me today," Charlotte told Winnie. "I will read about ruins on a less beautiful day."

"Alas, my grasp of Coptic is not so strong as yours." Winnie looked skyward, to the vast blueness interspersed with picturesque white clouds, and sighed. "I shall keep to my original schedule."

Charlotte breathed an inward sigh of relief. She loved Winnie dearly and enjoyed her companionship in almost all things. But as one grew, one acquired secrets and a greater need for privacy. With the canny manipulation of her schedule, it was possible to avoid spurning her friend outright or engaging in difficult conversations.

She felt some regret as Winnie walked away, not merely for losing time with her friend but for her missed studies. Charlotte enjoyed the subject and took heart from Miss Murray's work within the archeology department. Perhaps she, too, might assist the faculty or publish her own papers.

Until quite recently, Charlotte had planned to find some way to work in the field in Egypt.

She had wondered aloud to Edward, once, if such studies might be of use, since the Order's symbols were based upon those of ancient Egypt. He had gently disabused her of such notions before she could embarrass herself in front of the others.

Her face burned to think of the conversation now, and she supposed that he was correct to suggest that she ought to become an initiate of higher level mysteries before undertaking such work. Perhaps after additional study—and earning her university degree—she might revisit the idea.

Charlotte mounted her bicycle. It was a rather lovely standard model and she felt quite proud to ride it. She prodded the right pedal and found it remained tight after her repairs the previous week. Though she might not possess the mechanical skills of the fictional Miss Anastasia Welsh, Charlotte took care to bicycle prepared, with extra screws. Maintaining the contraption made it feel more hers, a vehicle she used to travel where she would, rather than a fashionable gift from her father.

The pedal, and the rest of the machine, performed beautifully as Charlotte made her way through the streets of Bloomsbury. Even without the meeting, perhaps this would have been a day best spent outside the library. Although Charlotte would have gladly ridden in rain or sun, she appreciated the good weather. She did not wish to appear at Edward's door wet, muddy, and bedraggled. Her youth and newness to the Order of the Golden Tyet were cause enough for insecurity without adding personal slovenliness.

Was this, perhaps, the reason Edward had told her to wait before traveling abroad? A magician might do better to think independently about her craft before traveling across the world, with a research agenda set by someone else.

Charlotte parked her bike by Edward's Marylebone townhouse and took a moment to work upon her presentation. She buttoned her split skirt and did her best to tuck in wisps of hair dislodged during her ride. She was not especially pretty, but had a pleasant enough face that was improved by looking properly put-together. At least, that was what her mother advised (the second part, at any rate; she had never intimated Charlotte was anything less than lovely). With a final, deep breath, she presented herself at the door.

Edward opened it himself. This was no surprise—she had never seen staff at his home, and supposed he dismissed them for the times when meetings were planned. Still, she felt a small thrill at the impropriety of the situation. He, no less than she, was moving in the shadows to avoid society's disapproval. So were all the others who met at this house. That, no less than their shared interest in magic, bound them together.

Edward was forty or so, she guessed: young enough to appear quite virile, but old enough that one could see where greater age would mark his face. She rather liked the way his smile crinkled the corners of his eyes, and did not think his temples or mustache suffered from the addition of a smattering of gray hairs.

"Miss Montgomery," he said. "What a pleasure it is to see you. Do come in."

Charlotte smiled back and offered a curtsy in a shared mockery of formality. "Mr. Fitzgerald."

But not a moment later, she had to stifle dismay at the sight of four men and two women already settled into the sitting room. Charlotte had expected to arrive early, not be the cause of delay. The others were all too well-mannered to comment on her tardiness, offering smiles or nods of acknowledgement to the newest—and youngest—initiate. Forgiveness and fellow-feeling might be expected among members of the same Order, but Charlotte was nonetheless relieved.

"Now that Charlotte is here, we may begin," Edward announced and, with a small bit of ceremony, unlocked the cabinet.

Charlotte's stomach roiled with gratitude that they had waited for her and anxiety that it had been necessary. These were not the emotions one should carry into a spell casting. And it appeared that they would, in fact, begin with the spellwork rather than the philosophical discussion that sometimes opened the Order's meetings.

Edward had withdrawn candles and the large, hand-bound book: a painstaking collation of practical and theoretical magical knowledge. Several elaborate bookmarks were sewn into the binding, used to mark sections appropriate for different levels of initiation. So far as Charlotte knew, only Edward ever touched the book in more than the most incidental manner; she had never seen anyone else open it or turn the pages. She wondered if she was alone in gauging how many pages remained at higher levels of initiation, and when she might see them.

Edward set the book in its place on an ornately carved table, Charlotte drew the curtains, Miss Alexander and Mrs. Williams positioned the candles, and the remaining gentlemen moved the furniture. The space prepared, they covered their clothing in ceremonial robes—simple garments, even Edward's, intended to erase the distraction of fashionable dress and adornment. In this space, they were all the same, all magicians on a path toward enlightenment. If some of them were farther along that path than others . . . well, everyone began somewhere.

Charlotte took deep, calming breaths. She was nearly used to the weight of the robes, so much more awkward than her own clothing, which had been tailored to accommodate her body's movements. But these robes were ritual tools, and mastering any tool required practice.

Charlotte stepped into her place in the circle. Her awareness of her fellow initiates expanded. She might not know details of their lives—the character of all their family members, the magazines they read, their favorite foods, the way they had found the Order—but she knew they were here, now, with her. They traveled the same path and trusted one another along that journey.

The written instructions were agnostic as to what one chose to look at, or not, during the ceremony. Charlotte had experimented at past meetings and so closed her eyes with confidence. The red-black veil comforted her. As the seconds passed, the colors shifted and wove together. Cocooned within her own body, she could sense the presence of otherworldly energy and saw those woven strands writhing, seeking contact. She urged them in the direction of the other bodies, other souls, within the room. Quite abruptly, she sensed her fellows much more clearly as they were bound together by strings of energy delicate as tissue and eternal as the earth.

As one, Charlotte and the Order began to chant.

∽ • ∾

When the working was done, Edward spoke about how their small voices spun together to make a greater whole. "We are told to think of ourselves as separate creatures—creatures who might cleave to one another or feel the warm bonds of friendship or family, but separate nonetheless," he began. "But this is a sterile, simplistic view of our potential," he continued. "*I* is an infinitely lonely and limited thing. We can transcend this cage, this lie that we have all been taught, and such transcendence is both a prerequisite and reward of mastering magic. It is through our will that we can reach out, through our will that we can find one another. . . ."

Charlotte let the words wash over her. She could still feel her brethren. They glowed with inward light—a heat that reached out to her, more diffuse but no less real than the strings felt during their chants. Did they feel the same force in her? She shivered in anticipation, for surely this awareness could only expand as she learned more of the Order's mysteries.

Her mind ought not wander to selfish concerns; she ought to pay attention to Edward's words. But her mind refused, instead turning his speech into a series of waves washing over her. It cooled her, dulling the radiance she felt from the others. She was floating in a sea, buoyed and enveloped.

And then it stopped. The others moved, spoke the ritual words dissolving the meeting. Charlotte reflexively copied them, her own words and motions delayed but not, she thought, awkwardly so.

The meeting's dissolution did not destroy her sense of the others, but the nature of their connection changed. She no longer felt submerged in water, but that vast medium now felt more akin to the night sky. Her fellows were distant stars she could observe but not touch. Was she as a star to them? How did a working feel to those privy to more mysteries?

They folded the robes, put away the candles, replaced the furniture, and opened the curtains. Edward left the book in its place, which was not at all his wont, and bid the others farewell. Charlotte trailed into the hallway, surprised to see the clock showed three hours had passed.

"Do please remain a moment, Miss Montgomery," Edward said.

Charlotte stood awkwardly in the hallway, wondering if she had made any ceremonial missteps. Under her concern were also feelings of gratitude, that she might have a few moments conversation with Edward, alone.

He was smiling when he faced her. "Dear Charlotte, I knew you belonged in the Order. Tell me, what did you feel today?"

"Connected," she said, and that spark-she-had-been burned again within her. "All of us in the room . . . we were bound together. Binding ourselves, one to the other."

His smile widened. She felt relief, not having thought herself capable of finding appropriate words.

"You may be ready," he said, and led her back to the room.

She could feel the faded glow of the ceremony, not wholly extinguished by the sea of Edward's closing words. Excitement coursed through her as he touched the book. When first initiated, she had felt completely unworthy to learn ancient secrets pieced together through study and meditation. Now . . . she still felt young but, after today's ceremony, it seemed appropriate that she learn more. Edward, obviously, agreed.

But she was still somewhat taken aback as he stroked the various bookmarks. He did not open the pages marked by the next one—which was, surely, the level of initiation immediately above her own. Instead, he opened the book to a point nearly three quarters to the end. Disciplined, she did not look at the pages without invitation.

"You're very active, not just young," Edward said. "You are in good health, and you ride that bicycle hither and yon. You clearly *inhabit* your body."

"Of course." She hid her confusion, unhappy to feel the *naïf* once more.

"Not everyone does, not fully. Whether through inclination or age or infirmity, many act as though the flesh is a prison to be escaped or transcended. But our materiality is a precious gift. A good magician is wise enough to use it as a tool as well."

Charlotte opened her mouth, about to speak on the value of the chanting, breath and flesh and language moving as one, strengthening one's own energy and the bonds between the group. She was about to say that she understood, and was eager to learn new rituals. But before she could, Edward nodded solemnly toward the book and, releasing a breath to calm her nerves, Charlotte looked upon pages devoted to advanced mysteries.

The sections of the book she was privy to were mainly text. A few diagrams accompanied descriptions of ceremonies, depicting where participants should stand and the proper orientation for casting. *This* section, however, was mainly pictorial in nature.

Only two magicians were depicted in the woodcuts. A man and a woman twisted their bodies together in ways that Charlotte knew should make her blush. She was a respectable young woman of the middle class—and suddenly conscious that she was unchaperoned in the house of a gentleman.

But her growing sense of wrongness had less to do with propriety and more to do with the impracticality of the illustrations. In one, the woman extended a leg at an unnatural angle that would require dislocation of the hip joint. The man's organ was quite large—Charlotte questioned the artist's grasp of perspective—and he bent his spine backward at an angle impossible for the human body. She did not see how anyone could correctly perform the rites.

And how did one go from ceremonies performed by the most inexperienced of initiates to *this*? As she participated in more complex spells with the Order, the positioning and movement of bodies became more subtle. Early ceremonies involved only four initiates, but after that the number increased, with each initiate increasing the strength of the spell. She did not see a natural progression from those workings to this . . . athletic repudiation of physiology.

She was conscious of Edward watching her reaction, a slight hitch in his breathing. She felt her puzzlement turn to a frown.

"I don't understand."

He smiled indulgently, his fingers covering hers. Belatedly, she realized she had touched the pages.

"I suppose it may be because I have not seen the intermediate mysteries," Charlotte continued.

Edward was very, very close to her. "I think you are ready," he said. "Do not tell the others; they may be jealous of your progress. Some take longer than others to learn the—"

She shook her head and captured hand—then turned the page, as though inspecting a book at the library rather than an object lately revered. "No, this isn't . . . it doesn't make *sense*." The next set of illustrations were engravings showing ever more complex positions and the introduction of a crook and flail, used in a manner not depicted in any Egyptian art Charlotte had studied. The nude figures acquired clothing of a sort, tight and impractical and somehow even less respectful of propriety than nudity.

"How does one breathe or move?" Charlotte felt her brow furrowing, as it did when she was intellectually stymied by a puzzle of archeology. Was this some sort of test to see if she had grasped the fundamentals of ceremonial magic? "If you fight your body—your clothes—your tools . . . that cannot help during a ceremony."

She turned another page and a half-tone photograph testified to modern practice. The faces of the man and woman were obscured by veils wrapped about head and limbs, which threatened to interfere with physical activity. Thick curtains had been hung as background—and, no doubt, obfuscation from the prying eyes of neighbors—and the pair perched upon an altar emblazoned with the symbols of the Order.

As Charlotte had surmised, pelvic bones did not allow the woman's legs to spread quite so far as earlier illustrations suggested was optimal. The man's partially-visible member was not so alarmingly large and his spine appeared intact. But they were clearly attempting a rite described earlier. Any resulting magical effects went unrecorded by the camera.

The limitations of photographic technology were not to blame, though, but rather the mannered flailing of the bodies atop the altar.

"This cannot possibly work."

Edward stared at her for a moment. "But, dear Charlotte, do you not wish to try?"

There was something in his voice—the huskiness, the sharp intake of breath—and sudden understanding burst upon her like heavenly enlightenment. His goals were not hers. He did not seek knowledge, particularly, though he may have acquired some along the way. His interest in her body, her mind, that burning spark she had felt during ceremonies, was fleeting and base. Not merely base, for she could not bring herself to condemn material pleasures. But his interests were *boring*.

She felt like a child. Not merely a foolish young woman, but a *child*, a naive seeker of knowledge. How could she have failed to notice his true interests? Her own breath unsteady, she simply said, "No. I thank you for the invitation, but I must decline."

This was the moment when a man might persist: many of the gentlemen in the stories she read had to make proposals more than once before they were accepted. For a long moment, he was silent, and she was suddenly very conscious of his greater strength and the fact that the house was deserted. A gentleman, she realized, was not the only sort of man who might persist.

But in the end, Edward smiled politely and stepped back. "Please do consider it as a future option."

She saw how it would be. He would ask, verbally or otherwise, whenever he saw her. She was less an initiate than a pending conquest. "I shall." Charlotte smiled politely and made an exit that felt like a retreat. His words of praise, cherished until now, turned to ash.

Shame burned her cheeks and tears threatened. Had he misread any heat as embarrassment or passion? Perhaps. But if such a misreading allowed her to leave more quickly, she could not think it a bad thing; and there was some satisfaction in the thought of having hidden her true feelings.

Outside, she undid the buttons on her skirt. It was no less a tool than the robes or candles she had lately mastered. The garment allowed her to move, to use her body to operate a machine that propelled her forward. And, today, it allowed her to escape.

She touched the standard's handlebar with affection and mounted the bicycle, riding away from Edward's for the last time.

She regretted her foolishness and almost every conversation she had ever shared with Edward. And yet, she ached for the loss of what knowledge the Order possessed. What other non-pornographic diagrams and ceremonies might have made their way into Edward's book? The spellworkings were real: she had felt her senses open beyond the physiologically possible and her consciousness expand.

Reminded of their earlier warmth and glow, she also ached for the loss of the other members of the Order. Had she been deprived of a community or were they and Edward all of a piece?

She considered returning to the university library. Winnie might yet be there, diligent in her studies of ancient languages, a proven friend.

But Charlotte was not quite certain she was ready to face other people. Her body still sang with the energies of the ceremony. Nothing Edward might say or do could shake her certainty that magic existed and was within her grasp.

Detangling her interests from Edward's might not be easy, but her goals were important. It wouldn't surprise her if his dismissal of her desires to travel and pursue archeological fieldwork were motivated soley by his sexual appetites. Perhaps she should start there; embrace her earlier instincts and travel to Egypt for her love of learning, without the need to impress a questionable mentor.

Charlotte pedaled through London's streets, using her body and her clothing and her bicycle, all tools at her disposal. *Inhabiting* her body, as Edward had said. He was not wrong about everything, she decided.

She felt free, the city—the world—laid out before her. A place of beauty and history and mystery, a set of puzzles waiting to be studied and, perhaps, solved. At this moment, she rode astride a modern machine, but she was not the first to travel these paths. Roman soldiers had tromped through London; men from the capital itself to the farthest-flung corners of the empire. Saxons, Danes, Normans, part of a parade of newcomers stretching back millennia. This isle had been peopled when Egypt rose, built its great works, and declined. The signs of the Britons' lives were less grandiose than pyramids—barrows, henges, and stone circles— but no less part of the landscape. She had wished so strongly to go to Egypt, perhaps she had unfairly ignored what sat before her in England.

She was an English magician and an archeologist. Still studying—she would always be studying—but already practicing. She, alone, was enough; if she found like-minded seekers, so much the better, but she could choose her associates. There was much to learn, and many sources from which to learn.

Without conscious thought, she turned toward Regent's Park. It was a place one could be seen, but Charlotte was more interested in seeing. She released the handlebars, trusting in her sense of balance, and lifted her feet from the pedals. She closed her eyes, warm light painting her eyelids red.

Face raised to the sun, Charlotte coasted through the patch of natural world, held close in the heart of her city.

DAY OF THE DEATH COMPASS (A WITCHCANIX STORY)
✃ *M. Lopes da Silva* ✃

T wo witches stood at the edge of an enchanted forest, adjusting the straps on their backpacks and stomping their feet more firmly into their boots. It was so early in the morning that a thin mist dampened everything except the young witches' excitement.

"This is it," Marlo said, scratching the short brown stubble of her sidecut. "Are you ready? Got the map?"

"Right here," Betula said, patting her backpack.

"Backup runes?"

"You know it!"

"First aid kit? Sunscreen?"

Betula pouted, her purple pigtails slumping at an angle. "Why do you need first aid when you've got me around? I brought my wand."

She pulled out the wand in question from her pack—a short pine twig tied with dried palm fronds which anchored a lumpy piece of rose quartz to one end of it. Marlo frowned at the witch. Betula sighed and put her wand away.

"Fine, yes, I packed your first aid kit, too. It's in your backpack. *I'm* not carrying all those vials and liniments and things."

"I'm not saying that you're a bad healer or something, Bet." Marlo said.

"I know."

"But this Death Compass was expensive—*you* know how long I've been saving for it!"

"I know, I knoooooow." Betula said.

"And it's only got, like, three good charges before it dies."

"I kn—Wait. Only three? Really?"

Marlo felt her face get a bit warm. "I could only afford a used one."

"Well," Betula started, squeezing Marlo's shoulders. "I'm sure we'll find you a really good, dead animal in no time!"

"It sounds weird when you put it that way. I mean, it's accurate, but it's still weird."

"I'm trying to cultivate my vulture vibes today. Think like a scavenger!"

Marlo smiled at her friend. "I'm really glad that I met you, Bet. I wouldn't want to hunt dead magical critters with anyone else."

Now Betula smiled. A mourning dove hooted from one of the nearby trees. "So let's get corpse hunting already! How do you start this thing up?"

Marlo squinted at the Death Compass in her hand. It was cold and surprisingly heavy, considering that it appeared to be mostly made of bone. The exterior was that of a pocket watch but constructed of skull, and the bone face of the compass had a tiny, white, fly-like thing that sat upon its surface which Marlo eventually recognized as a broken fragment from inside a sand dollar. A small, nubby joint bone poked out where the winding stem crown on a pocket watch would usually be.

"Okay, so once I activate the spell and wind this part three times," Marlo said, pointing to the joint bone. "A charge is used up, and the compass should direct us to a dead magical creature in the forest. Pretty straightforward."

"Easy peasy," Betula replied.

Marlo hoped it would be. She took a deep breath, briefly rehearsed the words of the spell one last time in her mind, and began the incantation.

"Outta the way, witches!"

Marlo frowned. Those were certainly not the words of the spell. She turned around. A pair of knights at least twenty meters down the road clanked importantly towards them.

"We're not even *in* their way," Marlo muttered.

"Looks uncomfortable, doesn't it?" Betula said.

They stared at the two figures scrape-clanging down the path in their full armor. One of the knights carried a purple and gold banner that they dropped. Twice. The third time they dropped it, Betula felt bad and ran forward to help.

"No, no!" the knight scrambling in the dirt for her stick shouted. "The Knights of Walnut, Durham, and Jones do not need assistance from the peasantry!"

"Quit dishonoring my squire, you wicked witch!" shouted the other knight from behind the grill of his helmet.

Betula crossed her arms over her chest, her eyes narrowing. "Oh, I don't like being called that at all," she said.

Marlo ran up to Betula and grabbed her elbow. "Hey, why don't we just go stand somewhere else for a couple of minutes?"

Betula let herself be led away from the knights, but muttered her complaints to Marlo as she went: "Who's *rude* to a *witch*? I mean, who *does* that? You've got a runic welding torch now and that's as good as a wand—I bet we could hex them both into a pair of toasters. What do you think?"

"I think that, obvious ethics issues aside, hexing Royally Sanctioned Knights is probably a really quick way to get us into trouble with the Queen. We work at a junkyard, Bet, how are we going to raise bail funds?"

Betula shook her head. "Smart. You're always thinking ahead, Marlo. You're going to be great at running a witchcanic shop."

Marlo grinned a little.

"Have you got a license for that Death Compass?" the knight without the banner interrupted from behind.

"Of course," Marlo said, her grin falling away. "And we don't have to show it to you unless we're under arrest for suspicion of committing a crime against the crown."

A low whistle made its way out of the knight's helmet, which made Marlo think of a teapot. "Well, well, well—you certainly seem to know a lot about committing crimes against the crown," he said.

"No, but I do know a lot about the laws concerning Death Compass use. Because I'm about to use one."

The knight glared at Marlo imperiously through his protective grill. Presumably, the squire glared through hers as well, but her visor only had a thin horizontal bar to glare through so it was difficult to tell.

The knight nodded at the enchanted forest. "There's been some poaching going on. You two wouldn't happen to know anything about it, would you?"

"No," Marlo said, "we just got here."

"Well, if you see anything suspicious, you be sure to report it to a knight."

"Right, well, Sir— I don't know your name— "

The knight drew himself upright noisily. "Sir Gregorith of Dunderglen and The Associated Knights of Walnut, Durham, and Jones, and Dame Anna the Unpromoted."

Betula looked like she wanted to ask something, but stopped herself from saying a word.

"Okay Sir Gregorith, may we get on with our spell?" Marlo asked.

The knight pointed an armored finger at her. "Try not to commit any crimes while you're out there. You're dismissed!"

Now Betula had to tug Marlo away by the elbow.

∽ • ∾

As soon as Marlo gave the winding crown its final turn, the fly-like bone lit with iridescent magic and flew towards the northeast edge of the compass face. The witches tromped through the forest together, steadily following the direction that the sand dollar fragment indicated while trying to avoid trees and large rocks.

"You're finally going to get your witchcanic shop!" Betula enthused.

Marlo held up her hands defensively and smiled. "Let's not get ahead of ourselves. We don't even have anything to work with yet."

"But you've got a Death Compass, and a runic welding torch, and me! That's basically everything you need right there."

"Basically!" Marlo laughed. "But we still don't have, like, an investor. Or a shop. Those are kind of important."

Betula waved some ivy aside. "Oh, you'll get all of those once they see how good you are at making stuff. What are you thinking of making, anyway?"

Marlo shrugged. "Well, don't laugh at me, but I was thinking . . . maybe bikes or something?"

"You really like bikes a lot, huh?"

"I like coming up with the frames the most. Designing something that fits a client and their needs just right. Lighter frames for people who need the speed. Heavier frames for those who need the support. I want to make bikes for everybody, Bet. Folks who can't ride normal bikes and need something special—I like figuring out how to make that happen." Marlo fell silent, distracted.

"You don't have to stop talking. I think that's really something special—"

"No, look!" Marlo interrupted, holding her hands out.

The Death Compass sparkled more intensely, dazzling the witch's vision with shards of light. They took stock of their surroundings. Just beyond the underbrush, they could make out a basilisk on the path.

The basilisk's long, snake-like body writhed in the leaves. Foam dripped from their beak. Their rooster legs slowly pedaled in the air while their tiny dragon wings thumped against the ground.

"It's alive!" Betula said, holding a hand over her mouth. "I thought that a Death Compass only led you to dead things!"

Marlo frowned. "It seems like the compass led us to a dying magical creature instead of a dead one? But it shouldn't have done that. I guess—"

Betula already had her wand out. The rose quartz tip sparked pink, and the basilisk shuddered. A moment later, the basilisk's legs found purchase on the ground and it sat upright. Flapping its wings to settle them back into place, the animal clucked a couple of times before preening itself.

"Well. I guess you could heal the basilisk. That's one option." Marlo said.

℘ • ℘

"Are you mad?"

"I'm not mad." Marlo said.

They were venturing southeast this time. There were a lot of tree roots to trip over along the way.

"Promise you're not mad?"

"I promise I'm not mad. We've got two charges left, we're doing fine."

"I just couldn't help myself. I can't watch suffering and just *not* do something." Betula said.

"I know. I'm not mad. The Death Compass wasn't working right for some reason. I've double-checked the spell and the runic connections. This charge should work."

Betula smiled. "I knew you'd understand. This time will be great—you'll see! And then we'll have sandwiches. I made you a cucumber one!"

As Marlo grinned back, the Death Compass sparkled with the same dazzling intensity as before. They paused, squinting as they scanned the underbrush up ahead.

A tinny, piteous roar split the air, and Marlo gave a small groan. A purple dragon about the size of a cat struggled on the ground. Pale foam formed at the edges of its mouth.

"Look, it's not like I want to see the dragon die. Nobody wants to see that. But maybe," Marlo began as Betula reached for her wand.

"Maybe. . . ." Marlo continued sadly, "it was its time to go?"

But Betula already had a spell zinging pinkly through the air. Within seconds the dragon shuddered, then yawned and stretched. They began kneading the leaves of the forest floor with gentle crunches, their purr loudly reverberating among the trees.

∽ • ∾

The two witches ate their sandwiches in silence.

"You're mad. I know it. This time—I'm pretty sure." Betula said.

"I'm annoyed." Marlo said. "I'm frustrated. And I'm starting to reconsider some recent decisions that I've made."

"Like what?" Bet asked nervously.

Marlo sighed. "Like buying a used Death Compass. Maybe I should've saved up for a new one. Or better yet, saved up enough to buy a legal kill from a knight."

Betula sighed too. "I'm glad that's what you were reconsidering. I was worried that you might've been regretting bringing me along."

Marlo smiled. "I don't regret much in life, and I'd never regret having you around."

Betula's face flushed with warmth. "I want to help you start up your witchcanic shop, Marlo! I want to help you build beautiful, weird, cool bikes and stuff. Not only is it your dream, but doing this with you is the most fun I've ever had."

Marlo frowned. "No. Wait. I mean yes, it is my dream. And I love doing this with you, too." She shook her head. "But none of that is what's bothering me right now."

"So what is?"

"Well, weren't both of those critters dying in a pretty similar way?"

"Before I healed them, yeah," Betula said.

Marlo nodded. "Exactly. They were both moving slow and odd on the ground. Disoriented. And there was foam coming from their mouths."

"Do you think they were both sick with something?"

"Sick, or poisoned maybe."

"Poisoned!" Betula was shocked.

"Those knights did mention poaching. A poacher might use something unethical like poison if they knew that their client couldn't tell or wouldn't care." Marlo finished off her sandwich, then returned the wax paper to her backpack and clapped her hands clean of crumbs. Betula stared at Marlo, still aghast.

"Just a thought for now, though. Well. Let's see if the third time really is the charm."

They followed the Death Compass north. The morning mist had long burned off, and odd sunlit oblongs dotted the forest floor. Fairies giggled and hid among the highest tree branches, always far out of reach.

"Do you really think that those animals were poisoned?" Betula asked.

"It could explain the problem with the Death Compass. Atomic constellations of magical creatures have been known to warp spells if they're dislodged from their bodies before they're able to accept their own deaths. That's why even legally sanctioned hunts are so expensive—offerings to spirits have to be made. Local animal populations have to be respected. It's complicated." Marlo stopped in her tracks. "Wait, do you hear that?"

"Hear what?"

"I think it's running water."

It was a small brook, half-hidden by a floating skin of pine needles. It was noticeably cooler standing even a few meters away from the water. The brook was so charming that for a moment the witches didn't even notice when the Death Compass began to sparkle again. They saw the firebird first.

The firebird's plumage glowed and shifted just like flames; at first Marlo thought that they'd spotted a phoenix. But the firebird was not truly on fire—its plumage was an optical illusion. One that was flashing in and out of visibility.

The firebird was hopping erratically in the mud, screeching in misery. A little foam fell from its beak, just like the basilisk and the dragon.

Marlo didn't even bother protesting. Within minutes Betula had removed her wand and returned the firebird to full health.

೮ • ೮

Marlo paced in the small clearing where they'd found the firebird. "Okay," she said, "so we think that the magical creatures were poisoned. All of them shared similar symptoms."

"And they were all smallish," Betula said helpfully. "It's not like there was a hippocampus or something in there."

"Right, maybe they were being turned into bicycles for fairies. A pixie fixie scheme."

Betula crossed her arms over her chest. "Really?" she asked.

But Marlo wasn't paying attention, having spotted something in the mud. She crouched down and began swiping at the dirt before removing a small white object.

"I have no idea. The sizes could just be a coincidence," Marlo finally responded. "But I *do* know that some knights from Walnut, Durham, and Jones have been by recently."

"How do you know that?"

Marlo held up the white object she'd found—a limp paper rectangle with a purple and gold design on one side—neatly printed with Sir Gregorith of Dunderglen and Dame Anna the Unpromoted's names on the other.

∽ • ∾

The two witches crouched in the thick cover of some wild roses on the far side of the brook.

"Why would those tin can cops want to poison magical creatures? They're allowed to kill them anyway!" Betula whispered.

"That's true—the knights are the only people legally allowed to kill magical creatures, but it's expensive and requires a lot of paperwork if they want to do it the right way. The thing is, they also get some pretty high demand from fancy chop shops with wealthy clientele. I wouldn't be surprised if there's more than one knight who's decided to bend a few rules for some gold on the side."

"Do you really think they'll come back here?" Betula asked, nervously.

"Well it's late afternoon right now. If they don't come by, I guess we just set up camp and head home in the morning."

"And then what?"

"And then on Monday we go back to the junkyard, and I start saving up all over again."

"*We* start saving up. I want to be your business partner, Marlo!"

"We start saving up," Marlo said, smiling. "Wait, I think I hear something—"

ᔇ • ᔆ

"I don't get it," said Dame Anna the Unpromoted. "The baits were all taken, but there's no bodies."

"Maybe those witches got to them first," Sir Gregorith said. "I thought the poison would give us more time to collect the creatures. Curse those alchemists—they always try to cheat you on potency!"

Marlo stood up from her hiding place behind the wild roses, snapping the spell on the runic welding torch to life with a hard flick of her wrist.

"I think I've heard enough," she said.

And then the torch went out.

"Oh, come on," Marlo said. "The welding torch, too?"

As Marlo stood there, flicking her wrist and muttering to herself, Sir Gregorith drew his sword.

"Charge!" he cried.

At the command, Dame Anna the Unpromoted lowered her banner like a javelin and lunged, the pointy-side aimed at the witch's heart.

Pink light zigzagged from the underbrush, catching the javelin mid-lunge. As Betula's magic connected with the javelin's wood, the weapon began to branch and sprout leaves. The banners tore away. Abruptly, Dame Anna the Unpromoted held a small tree in her arms. She fell over.

Sir Gregorith leapt over Dame Anna's struggling form, brandishing his broadsword. "I'll sell your witchy bones for scrap!"

One of Marlo's wrist flicks caught, the runic welding torch lit up. "There we go!"

Sir Gregorith's blade descended, quickly. Marlo grinned, and the white light blazing at the end of the runic welding torch flared up and sparked rainbows. The light saturated the forest, freezing them all in glittering aspic. The light broke things apart, cut, burned, and began to make something new.

"Wow," Betula said. "I didn't think you'd actually turn them into toasters."

"What can I say? You inspired me."

Betula laughed. "But your investor, your proof of concept . . . how are we going to get you supplies to make a bike now?"

Marlo shrugged. "I guess we can see how much these toasters go for, and start from there."

"You sure you're okay with that?"

"What do you mean?" Marlo said.

"Well, it's going to take longer to get to your dream of opening a shop."

Marlo smiled. "That's okay. I've got a partner now. We can get there together, one toaster at a time!"

And they did.

CHARMS
✌ Hester Dade ✌

The rain started the moment I stepped outside. As soon as my foot touched cobblestone, a droplet fell in mimicry. With my second step, another. Then, as I began to run, the pace of the rain increased in kind as I skittered to the shelter of the bike shed. On the final step, something squeaked.

Emboldened now that I was under the plastic roof, the rain beat a steady march. I lifted my foot to investigate and, yep, there was a smog mote trying to wriggle out of the tread. I pinched it and held it under the shower until it washed away.

Nasty wee things, smog motes. Not their fault, mind, but they needed clearing all the same. Checking the shelter for more, I found a dozen or so hunkering down in the cracks of the pavement. Each spun, resembling fuzzy acorns. These were small enough that all it took was shuffling them outside and the rain took care of the rest.

I found my bike and grabbed Sage's rucksack. Charms jingled in my pocket. Checking the time, I noticed there was still four hours before their gig started.

That gave me a few minutes to weave magic over all who parked here. I had a whole bundle of charms prepared and ready to roll. Some were objects I'd found: reflective bands, stickers, seat covers. Others were handcrafted; a little string of beads I'd made, all imbued with protection. A flash of lightning lit up my favorite, a cartoon hedgehog promising to protect whichever wheels they adorned.

One by one, I went to each bike and attached the charms. As each one snapped into place, a subtle ringing of alloy confirmed the charm had awoken. Spells were not my forte—I couldn't get my head around cleansing or healing magic—but protective charms I could do. They weren't elegant and they weren't powerful, but they did the trick.

Sage's rucksack weighed heavy on my back. How a person needed quite so much makeup for a five-minute routine, I'll never know, but they needed it and I was nothing if not a dutiful pack-mule—I mean partner. Tonight they would soar. I'd packed tissues and they'd packed waterproof mascara; I always cried at these things.

I took out the hedgehog and attached it to a stranger's front wheel, breathing the words to bring out the magic preservation of life.

Someone had left their headlamp on. I leaned over to turn it off. Before I touched it, the light went dark, only to flash back on with the roar of thunder. Flash-flash-flash, fl-a-ash. I turned it off, but there was no change, just repeating ragged flashes.

I watched the headlamp flashing until it repeated the pattern. It looked *deliberate*. It couldn't be. Could a bike be flashing a code at me? More likely I was seeing patterns where there were none. I looked around the shed for a camera or a hidden prankster, but I was alone.

I tried to film the flashing with my phone, but the camera couldn't pick up the changing lights. Not really sure what to do, I wrote the pattern out. It certainly looked like Morse Code. My dad had once said that seasoned code-breakers started hearing Morse in everything around them that clicked. He said he found one fellow having a conversation with a vending machine. Here I was transcribing a headlamp.

The headlamp finally blinked out, and I noticed how dark it was in the shed. I could solve the code later, but for now I had a bag of goodies to deliver.

I should have kept one of the seat covers to use as a rain jacket. Cradling Sage's bag from the storm, I scrambled back outside, past another line of bikes and a sign which welcomed folks to: "*Spoke friend and enter*".

A penny farthing sat conspicuously near the entrance. It looked decorative, like something to lure tourists in. Even in the rain someone was taking a selfie with it. I would have recognized that thing anywhere: the faint chalk marks on the spokes, the ribbons of baby blue, baby pink, and white wrapped over the handlebars, the cat-shaped reflector from my own collection perched on the front wheel.

What were the chances of seeing smog motes, a talkative headlamp, *and* the penny farthing on the same day? As much as I loved to see the owner of the anachronistic bike, it was rare for her to venture outdoors for pleasure. So if she was in town, something was afoot.

Unaware of the piling mysteries, Sage waited at the doorway. They were half-suited and half made-up, waving their hands at my arrival. They had applied a base layer of pale foundation, so they looked more Marie Antoinette than drag king.

I gave a flourish and offered the mostly-dry rucksack. "Your weapons, my liege."

"Cheers, babe." Sage peered out at the storm, then back at me. "You're drenched! I'm the worst human. Your coven friend is here by the way."

"Imogen, darling! Good morrow!" Hortensia's signature cadence came through from the community center.

"I gotta dash." Sage stepped forward and gave me a chaste peck. "Show starts at eight!"

For what it was worth I tried to dry my shoes on the mat before heading over to see Hortensia. Part repair shop, part café, part community space, the Three Wheels co-op had taken over the city's old fire station. They'd kept the large twin doors out front, but no pole sadly. Broken Wheel, the community area and home of the local coven, was 'round the back. The way a plain space could transform from cafe to theater to occasional marketplace was magic unto itself.

Hortensia was sitting beside a mostly-constructed stage. Despite the fact that she always drank mochas, she held the antique teacup she always carried in her purse, complete with matching saucer. Her perfume hit me before I was even close, a musky affair reminiscent of smoking parlors in manor houses. In a litany of skirts and petticoats, she was a force to be reckoned with. She looked timeless and powerful; each silver curl and crinkle at her eyes, each sunspot forming between dark freckles, was her visage reverting to form.

"Imogen, my dear, absolutely charmed to see you, it's been too long." She took a sip of her drink, her jewelry singing softly with the movement. "I thought you said you couldn't sense the barrier?"

The barrier. My stomach sank. Her arrival wasn't a coincidence. Something was wrong. One check of my phone fitness tracker and, yep, I saw Zara winding a route towards the next street over.

This was an impromptu meeting of the Broken Wheel coven.

The protective spell cast over the city must be waning. That would explain how the motes were wriggling in and the strange flashing lights. Although we were due to recast it in a few weeks, I hadn't the faintest clue it was failing this early.

"Hi." Zara arrived, turning from a dot on my GPS into the handsome woman smiling at me through the window. She walked her bicycle beside her with an easy confidence, her movements elegant and purposeful. All muscle, Zara wore her hair cropped short and dressed entirely in non-branded sportswear.

If I'm honest, I was utterly intimidated by her when we first met. I remember trying to sidle over to my bike to hide the basket and the painted flowers and the bright pink bell with a hummingbird on it. They felt so silly compared with hers; as the engineering instructor at the co-op, every nut and bolt of her bike was tuned to utility.

Back then she had tilted her head and said, "It's cute. Are those violas?" as I had spluttered three greetings at once.

As I did now. "Hellowareyouall-right?"

Smog motes, I can handle. River wisps, sewer fairies, alley pixies, all of these were fine. Other people? Now that was where I struggled.

"Good thanks, yourself?" Zara relaxed into the third seat. Her features were sharp and refined, her movements poised and thoughtful. Under the gray light of the storm, her light skin caught cool blue tones. She was the moon to Hortensia's sun. "Oh, Hortensia, did you knit that shawl yourself? Looks great."

"But of course! Thank you, my dear." She gave a bashful shrug. "I saw your editorial last week."

The two witches could not look more diametrically opposed. Where did that leave me? If they were the sun and the moon, I was Pluto. A puppy trying to remember more than a single spell, talking to plants in an attempt to feel closer to nature. Ever since

I'd joined them after one of Zara's lessons, dressed like a children's tv presenter, I had felt out of my depth with magic stuff.

"Are those your charms out front?" Zara asked. "You're getting good! I can feel them even sitting here. And once you've gotten the hang of a few spells, you won't need those."

"Bravo, darling." Hortensia finished her coffee and placed her hand on my shoulder. " I can see they're setting up everything for tonight. How exciting! Your beau's stage debut!"

"'*Life's a drag*'." Zara nodded, phone in hand. She showed me Sage's flier. "Sit tight and relax. We've got this. No worries."

Re-affirming the seal took a lot of energy. Technically the two of them probably could do it alone, but they'd be on bedrest for a week afterwards. I'd been a trainee for too long; it was time for me to start asserting my skills. "You can't get rid of me that easily." I affected a casual air. "A recast shouldn't take too long."

"Hm." Zara folded her arms. "If you insist. Strange for the barrier to falter so soon. I checked with the other chapters and no one else is reporting issues."

"There was one thing I noticed today, I think," I spoke slowly, unsure whether I should raise the topic or not. "I saw a bike flash Morse code at me? Is that something you've ever heard of?"

Zara's forehead creased. "I've heard of dodgy lights."

"Back in my golden years," Hortensia spoke as though she'd actually been alive then, "there was much hullabaloo over ghosts in radio. Spirits used them to channel warnings. What did this light say?" She read the transcription on my phone. "Danger hill. How curious."

By then the beating of rain had turned into a downpour, and the hunger in my stomach to trepidation. Now that I was aware of the spell waning, I could start to feel something growing around us. Cement paths began to bubble and buckle.

"A *headlamp* told you this?" Zara asked incredulously.

"I think so?"

"Alright." She said, and I was waiting for the inevitable moment she called me nuts. "We best take extra care around hills then."

The spell was waning, and with it, the city's protection against pollutants. It began as an acrid taste in the mouth. Harmless enough, but it would build and build. Smog motes would pool in every crevice of the city, creeping through cracks in doorways to spite homes, sinking into grates and waiting to pounce. Once a few had gotten in, they could multiply like nobody's business. They nested in lungs, making people cough and sneeze black from breathing city air. That was bad enough, but I'd heard that if they started building up they could morph into even worse beasties that went bump in the night.

In order to rebuild the barrier and stop the pollution, we would each ride to the highest points in the city; the hill of North Park, the terrace of the new shopping mall, and the tower of the old castle-turned-tourist-attraction. With our wheels active, we would each draw our lines over the city and culminate in an incantation spoken by all three of us at the same time. "When the night bell tolls," as Hortensia put it.

It was my role to trace the old city walls, redrawing the lines laid down by so many people before me. Zara had an encyclopedic knowledge of the city's roads; she had worked out the fastest routes, taking into account closures and building works. *Danger hill.* It made sense. I would be riding to the hill in North Park. There would be danger.

Under an awning, while people scarpered from the weather, we drew our runes. These were simple dots on the spokes that came to life like an old animation zoetrope when the wheels spun.

I drew mine in coloured chalk; it didn't make a difference, but it was more fun that way. I was still getting the hang of drawing chalk on metal, and had to redraw the marks a few times to make them visible. My lines circled around a reflective animal menagerie: an orange tiger sitting next to a green frog, fish poised to swim circles on the spokes, and a hamster waiting at the bottom, ready to run another lap. There were also two fancier reflectors shaped like butterflies I'd found at a crafts fair.

Hortensia's runes were decorative and elaborate, pieces of art in their own right. Zara kept the lines succinct, breaking the spell into its barest, purest structure.

We finished at the same time. I lifted my bike and gave the front wheel a spin. As it whirled to life, multi-coloured lines merged together as the spokes appeared as one. Circles, triangles, patterns all burst to life, transforming into complex patterns and letting out a low glow.

We all donned our helmets like knights of old. It didn't matter how many times I'd seen Hortensia weave her magic, her ridiculous historical bicycle always gave me pause. As the front wheel was considerably larger than the back, she crunched three spells into one wheel and the last into the smaller.

"Are you sure you can make it to the top of the castle with that thing?" I eyed it warily. It looked like it could fall apart at any moment.

"Oh ye of little faith." Even Hortensia's helmet had frills. "Come, ladies, the time to ride is nigh!"

Zara took out her phone and pressed 'Start'.

∽ • ∾

We rode together for a while. Hortensia somehow kept up with us despite her unwieldy steed and her leisurely demeanor. It was always such a joy to see the incantations at work, the white chalk lines forming spells across the wheels. Rain splashed up around us like halos.

Then we split; Zara took the first turn, Hortensia the second, and I the third. We left light trails in our wake. These would draw the lines for the purifying ceremony.

There were more cars out than usual, sleek and sliding through the growing dark. Smog motes clustered at the rims to avoid the weather. Orange lights reflected along the road. It looked like the ground was fading beneath us, leaving only water in its wake.

The route took me uphill. Two hills, to be precise. The words *danger hill* repeated over and over in my head. With the rain coming and my energy already draining out for the spells, it was brutal. At least there was a section in the middle where I could rest and let the bike take me along.

There were people I knew who loved hills, who actively sought out the tallest and steepest. I was not one of them. By the time I reached the top I couldn't tell which parts of my soaked clothes were rain and which were sweat.

At the crest, I caught up with a black hatchback waiting at the lights. Its rear wipers were dislodging smog motes taking refuge from the rain, flinging them off to the ground

A green light. I pushed off downhill, hands on both brakes, just as a new batch of motes were flung towards me.

Before I could react, the smog motes hit my front wheel and spun up to my handlebars. Several flew off, but some were caught in my brake levers. I couldn't stop my ride or the stream of obscenities that cascaded out of me. I couldn't brake. All the protection charms in the world couldn't help if I crashed at full speed.

My front tire slipped slightly. Just for a fraction of a second. Enough to remind me of my mortality.

The turn at the bottom came sharply into view. The old city wall. I couldn't brake and there was a wall. To the left was a space to walk down to the riverside.

The river in one direction, a wall in the other. I had to choose.

Stop, stop, stop.

Boots scraping across the ground, I felt every bump in the road as I desperately tried to stop. A purifying spell. There must be a quick one. Think, Imogen, think! Something to clean the mechanism.

Stop, stop, stop!

My teeth chattered until I finally found a spell in memory. A short incantation. Just eight words. I bit my tongue on the first syllable.

No one around me seemed to have noticed. No one saw the terror in my eyes. They were happily strolling about, without a care in the world, until—oh god—someone with an umbrella stepped out into the road.

Stop!

I brought my shoes down hard, just as I managed the final word. The mote was dislodged and the brake snapped down. The mote was sent careening into the air. As, unfortunately, was I. Weightless. I could see every detail as time stretched out before me. The woman with an umbrella apologizing. The droplets of water on her glasses. The dog at her side.

I bounced off the pavement like a rubber ball. I actually bounced. Then rolled.

Somehow I found myself sitting on the ground, stinging all over, but with everything intact. There was a bitter prickling all down my left arm and leg. I was aware of someone asking me questions. Was I alright?

Yes. Somehow. Beside me the river gurgled its threat and the wall was silent, but I was alive and between them.

A man had picked up my bike. "Good as new," he said, his confusion evident. "Are you okay to ride that thing?"

"It was, uh,"—I fumbled for the right words, so full of jitters that my entire body was shaking—"a magical obstruction? Mote in the mechanism."

"Magic?" He blinked twice, squinted, then shook his head. "Right. Sure thing. Magic," he said quickly. "You might need to replace your zoo though." Surrounded by the fading marks of the spell were broken pieces of cartoon tigers and frogs and fish.

When I'd first started casting, I'd kept the whole thing hush hush. But turns out you can say anything and strangers will just nod and move along. They had no idea what I was doing. No idea what the coven did, every moon, for years.

The pain shot up my side. I thought of how when I first signed up, Broken Wheel had me down on their books as a temp cleaner who would pop in on the odd weekend. I thought of Sage getting ready to perform. I could be off talking with them. I could be curled up indoors with a book. I could be *anywhere* except the side of a road with cuts down my side.

I'd need to renegotiate my rates after this.

The man started coughing. The woman knocked her chest to clear it. Even the dog started to hack. I could feel the approaching motes myself. They were gathering at the cracks in the pavement, in the shadows of passers-by.

There were more than I'd thought. Not even water could hold them off now.

There was no time. I had to get to North Park. My legs didn't look too scratched up. I could move my arms without pain, so that was something. I scuttled to my fallen bike and checked the runes. Hands shaking, I redrew them as quickly as I could manage. The lines were wobbly, but what wasn't in this city? I had my stash of pre-prepared charms to replace those that had broken. The handlebar needed adjusting, but beyond that my steed was looking very noble indeed. I grabbed the broken reflectors and shoved them in my pocket.

"Are you sure you should—" The woman said. Motes bubbled around her glasses.

There was no time.

I got back up and cycled towards the park. *Danger hill.* The message had come true. With that realization came a rush of relief. The danger was done. Yeah, I was bleeding but only a little—it looked worse than it felt.

Just one more hill, then I would be at one of the three highest points in the city. The movement sent jagged pain through my legs. Charms jangling by my hands, I continued to trace the purifying crest.

With the relief came a sense of pure joy. I'd faced the worst. It was only up from here. Crisp air filled my lungs and adrenaline flushed away my jitters.

It was some off-road cycling, not my area of expertise, but I could manage. I'd grown up in these woods, cut my cycling teeth, so to speak, on the forest trails. Once I hit my stride my mind was cleansed. It was just me, the wheels, and the air in my lungs.

Free. Ducking under leaves, bouncing over fallen branches, this was the moment that made it. Slowly, the city came into view as I climbed higher. Thousands of lights in the distance below dark clouds, the mall tower, the old castle walls. There was no word for it other than beautiful.

I saw it, the highest peak. Just as the bell tolled, I brought the spinning rune wheels to the focus point.

It lit from below, multi-coloured symbols rising to the sky. Breathless, I watched white lights shining from the castle and the mall.

Now, just the words to seal the spell. "We can do this!" I shouted into the night. The words didn't matter, it was the feeling. The knowledge that the city was imperfect, yes, that it was polluted and that the smog motes would be back within a month could be overwhelming. But if our efforts prevented a single accident it would be worth it. It would take a miracle to clear the airways completely, but a little magic couldn't hurt.

༄ • ༅

Pink lights scrawled our spell over the sky. I circled down and rode to the point where the rivers crossed. All around me, magic popped and rain washed away motes. Now that I didn't have to trace the spell lines, the return was much quicker.

Lights traced from the three highest points and joined in the middle before trickling down. I saw two cyclists approach the river as I did. One in professional gear, the other on a penny farthing. Together our spell illuminated around us. Falling rain glowed pink, orange, blue. The runes forming lines, falling to the ground like fireworks.

All except one line. It dwindled and fizzled.

I saw my confusion reflected in Zara and Hortensia's expressions. It didn't work. Or rather, it might be more accurate to say the spell *stopped* midway. It was faint, but I could feel something was stuck. As though our wires had been knotted along the way.

"Has this happened before?" I couldn't stop the panic leaking into my words. "What do we do?"

Hortensia and Zara looked at each other.

"Are any of the other chapters nearby?" Zara directed the question to Hortensia.

"Who?" I asked.

She shook her head. "Not to my knowledge."

"What?" I asked.

With a sharp curse, Zara took out her phone. "How is there no signal? I was just using it! Come on, come on, someone *has* to have felt this."

All I felt was lost. "What is happening?"

"Gremlins in the wire." Hortensia said. "Kobolds, imps, call it what you will. Something is blocking the spell."

That must have been the knot I felt, fleetingly, in the runes we had cast. Grateful as I was to finally start gaining intuition for magic, it wasn't time for celebrating. The old town bells began to ring.

"Can we, I don't know," I mumbled, "re-cast it?"

She crossed her arms. "It's no good, my dear. Not until we clear the obstruction."

I felt the hairs on my arm prickle, then there was a crackle in the air. I could definitely feel a knot, slightly out of reach, but there was no malice. It felt almost . . . *scared*. My front light began to flash short bursts and longer blasts.

"Hortensia!" I gestured for her attention. "The headlamp! It's Morse code! The same as before!"

The clock rang seven. Sage's gig was in an hour.

Zara frowned, watching the lights. "I think it's just broken. I'm going to ring the guys at Pendle."

The lamp grew dim before repeating the sequence.

Hortensia was very quiet. "I see! My dear, you said earlier it said 'danger hill'. It's not 'danger', it's badger."

Badger hill. I felt a pang of animal terror, caught the scent of musk and something acrid. The light flickered off.

Zara looked to me, then Hortensia, then to the headlamp. "There's a landfill site at Badger Hill. That could be causing issues if motes have built up there." She shrugged. "It's worth a try." She grabbed her bike, readjusted her helmet, then nodded upwards. "You two coming? I know a shortcut."

We rode as one. Now the motes were either being washed away or shuffling back into the drains.

It was just us, the road, and the wind.

∽ • ∾

With each passing road, that animal fear grew in my gut. Rounding the corner, the difference was clear. The spell was still trying to penetrate, but it was getting caught mid-air, congealing together with the mire.

Residential streets gave way to big box stores. The Badger Hill landfill loomed in the distance. The sign for the site was snapped in half.

Before we even pulled into the site, a horrifying sight was lying in wait for us: a beast of smoke towering over an upturned shopping cart and half a sofa. Smog motes gathered to form its slashing arms, growing from stacks of tires, the cumulative remains of a city's waste.

I was transfixed. I came to a stop as I tried to understand exactly what it was. There was the light clicking of my gear adjusting, and the other two witches halted beside me.

Then the smoke wrapped back around, snaking down a drainpipe. A person could be forgiven for mistaking it for woodsmoke. Not quite physical, swirling like rippling waves, whipping itself into a fury. It was beautiful.

Then its claws gouged lines through our spell. Its shape twisted into a snout with rows of dagger teeth. It let out a rumbling engine-like growl. The creature gouged lines in the spell with gray claws.

"What *is* that?" I shouted over the downpour.

"If motes are left to grow together, *that's* what you get." Zara gritted her teeth as the beast slashed through one of the perfect runes she'd made on the road. It sparked and trailed from the sky to the core. "We need to call in the Pendle witches."

"Zara, dear, we don't have time!"

The darkness clung to the beast and with every cut to our spells, there was nothing stopping it from growing even bigger. There wasn't time for debate.

I kicked off and rode straight for it. "A purification spell!" I turned sharply and traced the lines of our spell. The same as before, but on a smaller scale.

I ducked as the creature swiped at me. A tendril of it caught my rear wheel. One of my charms popped with a burst of light. Smog motes fell from the mass and were washed away in the rain. I was casting! I was actually casting!

Then the lights faded. My spell dwindled.

The beast pounced.

Darkness descended until it was all I could see. Its teeth caught around me, hot breath on my skin and whiskers splaying onto me. A fox catching a mouse.

In a moment it sloshed away with purifying rain. Hortensia's perfumed magic washed over me and through the beast. Motes which had formed the shape of fangs scattered and were cleansed in her spell. She couldn't hold it off for long.

Just as I peddled away, Hortensia's spell dropped. The beast stomped hard on the road. There was a loud crunch. Looking back, there was an indentation in the concrete where I had been standing.

All I could think was how my body might have reacted to an impact like that. The crunching sound echoed with the pulse thrumming in my ear. I remembered guiltily when I had first joined the Broken Wheel, Sage informed me that under no circumstances was I to engage in any reckless heroics.

"Imogen!" Zara's voice was strained. "That was unbelievably foolish!"

The beast let out a wail before turning to flee. It took lumbering steps away from the landfill site and towards the city. Something in that cry cut through my thoughts. It was the sound of something wounded, frightened. It left paw-shaped indentations.

"Yes, I know, I'm very sorry." I said quickly. "Are you *sure* that is just smog motes? It had teeth and whiskers and paws."

Hortensia was wiping her face with a handkerchief. "Imogen, my dear, please take care." Her nose was bleeding. "It did respond to purification, but I daresay we need a dash of teamwork next time."

"There is no '*next time*'. We are stopping immediately." Zara's phone once again rang out that she had no connection. "Oh, come on! We need back-up."

"My dear, speed is of the essence. We must cleanse that monster tonight." She patted Zara on the shoulder.

Zara grimaced, but knew she was right. "Fine."

"You and I shall cleanse it." Hortensia said. "Imogen, if you can, use your familiars to cast a net. Keep it contained."

Familiars? That was one way to describe my charms. "Okay," I agreed, and I swear the bell on my bike sang a little too.

Zara was the fastest; she circled around the beast and directed it back towards the landfill. It took a swipe and missed. Then Hortensia was at its flank and the pair were drawing their incantation lines across the road. Each time it turned towards the city, I wheeled around it. The reflective cat was the first to pop. Then the frog.

The spell finished. At each end of a triangle, we turned to face our enemy and spoke the words to seal it.

Lights shot from the ground and wrapped around it. Wherever it touched, motes were discarded and tumbled to the ground. The odor only grew as we made ourselves into a whirling circle and whipped the air into a froth.

A claw swung out and nearly struck Zara. The spell stuttered. Each time they tried, it lashed out.

"This isn't working." Zara panted after the third attempt. "We need something a bit stronger." She locked eyes with Hortensia. "Imogen, this *can* hurt you. Once I've drawn the lines you need to stay back. Everything within its circle is affected. Motes, yes, but also plants, animals, people."

The smoke gathered at a lamppost. It wrapped around it, smog motes reaching out in tendrils. As it rested, the ground around it started to shift and the post began to buckle. The beast was growing. The lamp burst into an explosion of more motes.

Hortensia nodded severely. "Stay back."

I cycled as far as I could without drawing the beast's attention. It was licking its wounds and increasing in size. The next lightbulb along cracked into a cloud of motes that fell to the ground.

The beast darted towards them. I caught a glimpse of its jaws closing around Hortensia, then she sent a jet of magic into its mouth. It spun away and tried to flee in the other direction, but Zara blocked its path. She, too, sent a spear of light into it.

An ear-splitting yowl echoed around the street. The yowl was so guttural it couldn't be smog motes. Motes don't feel pain, they don't feel anything. This clearly did. The teeth. The paws.

Zara and Hortensia sped in arcs as they traced the cleansing spell. It was drawn, all that was left was to cast it.

"Wait!" I shouted. That spell would affect every living thing; plant, animal, and person. This wasn't a monster formed entirely from motes. This was something else. "Don't!"

The confusion set Zara and Hortensia spinning off. The beast flailed and sliced through the spell lines. The two witches circled back to me.

"What are you doing?" Zara shouted.

"It's alive!" I pointed as it swung a smoggy claw, bending one of the parked bikes and leaving a pawprint on the concrete below. "Look!"

"We don't have time for this!"

The beast careened towards us. It collided with my back wheel. A spark burst from one of my charms. The pop cut through the beast's flank, sending a group of motes scattering. Underneath, I could just make out fur.

I didn't quite understand why, but the charms shifted the motes without hurting the creature within. The spell cast over the bicycle charms was for life preservation. This beast, too, was alive.

Charms jangled in my pocket. If we could trap it within a net of charms, the smog motes might just clear. I explained the idea as quickly as I could to the others. As I did so, I handed out as many charms as I could.

"Look. I trust you," Zara's face flickered between hope and fear, "but I promised Sage you'd return intact. We can try this *once*. Then we kill it."

"Where can I trap it?" I asked. "We need a dead-end and a bike rack."

"Two roads down." Zara said. "Outside the recycling centre. No one should be there at this time."

I nodded. "Give me two minutes, then drive it towards that road."

I didn't think I'd ever ridden that fast in all my years. Utterly soaked from the rain, my shoes were slipping off the pedals as I found the recycling center buildings. Two rows of bicycle racks lined the entrance.

The perfect space to trap a mote storm. I spoke the spell as I went, attaching seat covers and reflectors, whatever I had at hand. There was a reassuring jangling of frames as I laid each protective charm.

Then the beast came whirling towards the dead-end, my coven at its heels. It stepped right into the first batch of charms. They popped like fireworks. It roared. Zara pressed it further towards the bike rack. Each crackle elicited snarling, growling, whining.

Then a roaring from the beast. It tried to turn away, but Hortensia blocked the path. I hopped back on my bike to help with shepherding. We formed a line and gradually grew closer as it yowled and struggled against our defense.

The next lights fizzled, then the next. Motes were sloughing off it in droves. It stumbled as it shrank. A single black paw was visible under the smoke.

We pressed on. Another black paw. All the while lights reached in and cleansed the beast.

We were coming to the last line now. I could see a tail emerging from the mire. So close. Its cry rang in my ears. The last charms dispensed their magic. The beast shook its body and sent motes cascading. Orange fur underneath. It was so small now.

I let out a long breath. Everything hurt. My lungs, my muscles, my head.

The beast turned and leapt towards us. It wasn't clear. Smoke still clouded its head. I turned to chase it. We all did.

The beast bolted. So fast it could barely be seen except for the halo of rain at its paws. It ran straight out of the road—

—just as a man cycled past. A cartoon hedgehog on his wheel reflected the sight of the smog evaporating.

An ember lit as the spell burst between the beast and the stranger's bike. It was a matter of seconds, but it felt like time had slowed. The light remained suspended in the air as he narrowly avoided the beast. Smaller sparkles popped across the beast as its momentum took it through the spell. When the lights faded, a fox emerged from the mire.

It stepped over an indentation in the concrete and a line glowed beneath it. It was our barrier spell from earlier, this time with the obstruction removed. Lights rose to the sky and spread out beneath the stars.

Cleansed of motes, the fox's ears flicked towards us before it turned and trotted to the nearest hedge.

∽ • ∾

We snuck into the show through the backdoor and sank into the back row of seats. Sage was half-hiding behind a curtain to the side of the stage. They tapped their wrist—*what time do you call this?*—as the night's host ran through the show's ground rules.

"Beat our PB." Zara whispered with a smile.

We were all utterly soaked, a cloud of Hortensia's perfume fighting admirably to hide the smell of fox-landfill-monster.

When Sage stepped on, there was a moment where they took in my appearance; drenched, sweaty, probably torn up the arm now that I thought about it. But I was here, and they quelled a laugh.

Later, between sets, Hortensia held a mug of coffee high and declared a toast. "The newest fully-fledged member of Broken Wheel!"

Zara clinked her bottle of kombucha. "To the Broken Wheel and a toast to your success."

Jittery, I managed to take a sip of hot chocolate, holding back tears.. My entire body shook from a heady mixture of joy, anxiety, and a whole lot of exhaustion.

Hortensia just wrapped me up in her arms. "You kicked ass tonight, if you would pardon the expression."

"Couldn't have done it without you." Zara patted my shoulder. "Don't do anything like that ever again."

I laughed through the tears.We had faced uncertainty, doubt, and peril, but we'd come through it. I got the feeling this was going to be the first victory night of many—and I was going to need a lot more charms.

TOUCHING MARS
✍ *Monique Cuillerier* ✍

The sun is creeping above the horizon, its first feeble rays pierce the shadows in my bedroom.

I am awake and dressed, standing in the circle I cast.

A deep breath fills my lungs. I close my eyes and let the anxieties of the day empty from my mind.

Facing East, I focus on the element air. Air is the breath moving in and out of my lungs; air, representing my mind.

As my focus wavers, I turn to the South and allow myself to be consumed by the thought of fire, of energy, of will. It is strength coursing through me.

Then to the West, water, which flows over and around me, emotion and feeling.

And finally, North. The element of earth; my body, filled with silence.

I contain and encompass the entirety of the world, it is both part of me and held by me, very gently cupped in my hands.

This wasn't a ritual I performed growing up as a witch. I don't know if Agnieszka ever performed this or any rituals at all, actually. What I recall of her magic was very matter of fact, practical. The spells of daily life.

Then, she and my mom split up when I was still young. My mother was a witch, too, but non-practicing and my magical education was largely neglected between Agnieszka's departure and when I began to explore the craft for myself. But that was much later.

I owe Agnieszka a lot.

∽ • ⌒

In the first years I worked at the launch facility, the road to the campus was knotted with cars each and every morning. Actual, gas-fueled cars that would squat all day, unused, in the vast parking lots encircling the facility's collection of buildings and warehouses and hangars.

I rode my bike even then.

It wasn't very pleasant, of course, dodging and weaving amongst angry cars, belching exhaust, their engines emitting a constant, low-level whine.

There aren't any cars now.

Norma, who works with onboard power systems (the cute one with short dark hair and a thousand twinkling piercings), was the last holdout at the facility, although she had long since switched to a refurbished electric car. Eventually she gave even that up, the effort outweighing what it contributed to her image.

There is no gas to be had these days, and rechargeable batteries are in short supply. Using them for something as frivolous as a single-user vehicle is absurd.

Now, ribbons of bicycles thread across the wide road, sometimes intertwining, more often parallel, accompanied by a wave of happy chatter and random shouts.

So much is wrong with our world that it is easy to overcompensate and find extreme joy in the mundane.

∽ • ⌒

When I was first hired to work on the maintenance team, it was large and divided into sub-teams, each assigned to not only different buildings, but specific floors or wings. Back then, every office was full, each lab in use, in building after building after building. There were talks of expansion.

And then it began to fall away, bit by bit.

Fewer contracts, fewer staff, buildings were emptied and boarded up.

I've locked my bike in the same place, on the same rack I always have. Today is no different and I go inside, nodding to Marie at the security desk. My pass dangles around my neck, although she doesn't look at it.

The long hall I walk down ends at the entrance to the maintenance staff change room. I leave my bag there, cover my hair, and put on a fresh mask, thin jumpsuit, and shoe covers. Going into the central maintenance area, I check my cleaning cart to make sure the supplies are in order. These days it is only Clara and I in maintenance. I do the cleaning and she takes care of repairs.

Everyone—all the scientists and engineers, all the auxiliary staff—are in this single building now and, even so, it isn't full. Not even close.

I push the cart through the swinging doors and begin down the central hallway. Stopping at the first office, I open the door. No one is there, so I quickly collect the garbage and sweep the floor.

One office, then another. I make my way along the hallway until I reach the clean room, where our rover is being constructed right now.

I am also responsible for ensuring the clean room's pristine state is maintained, but that comes last, after everything else is done and I myself am re-sanitized and re-wrapped.

Regardless, I never pass by without looking through the window and saying hello.

"Good morning, Coda," I call out. She doesn't have an official name yet, but everyone has decided that Coda is perfect, the culmination of the work of generations.

While everything around us continues to fall apart, Coda will be sent to Mars. The last rover.

I worry, and I know it is silly and misplaced, about Coda being lonely once she leaves us. She has, after all, known nowhere other than this.

I know what it is like to experience loneliness. But I also know what it is like to feel its absence.

When I was a child, shortly before the last angry fight between Agnieszka and my mom, Agnieszka gave me the gift of comfort.

I had been having problems at school. I was nine or so and I didn't fit in. I never really did, but that year was harder than most. There was simply no place for me, no group I fit into, no individual friend, and, even worse, there were three girls who teased and mocked me relentlessly—for everything. That my mom was queer, although they didn't phrase it so politely, that we lived in a little house in the woods. That we were witches.

One of those days Agnieszka found me crying at the edge of our garden, where the forest began. I was leaning against a tree, watching the wind ruffle the leaves of the beans scaling the row of trellises. Focusing on their leafy greenness and trying to calm down.

It had been a particularly bad day. Two of the girls had followed me home from school, asking what was wrong with me, why was I so weird, shoving me, just a little, back and forth between them. Not enough to hurt me, but enough to make me feel out of control, enough to make me feel like there was no way out, no end.

Agnieszka didn't ask me what was wrong. Instead, she sat down on the grass beside me and waited until I was ready to talk.

When I was finished, she told me she could give me the comfort of her presence, all the time. Did I want her to do that?

I wasn't sure it would help, but it seemed like a nice idea.

We went to the room she used for work, the little one that opened off the landing between floors, and she took down one of her notebooks. Its cover had a design of deep green and purple. She flipped through the pages, stopping at one that was titled 'the comfort of a friend.'

I don't know if it 'worked', whatever that would mean, but there was a new sensation, like a warm pebble under the skin on the front of my right shoulder. I couldn't feel it when I examined the area with my fingers, but I had an awareness of its presence.

And I did not feel lonely the next day or the day after and so on.

After Agnieszka left, it was different, of course. The presence was still there, but the comfort began to eke away.

Perhaps without my presence in her life, she began to forget about me.

But all these years later, a small sense of someone being with me remained, as normal to me as breathing or eating.

∽ • ∾

"Hi, Edie, Clara," Norma says as she sits down with us in the lunchroom.

"How's it going?" I ask, trying, as always, to sound relaxed. So of course I don't. It's stupid for a fifty-four-year-old woman to have a crush on anyone, let alone someone twenty years younger.

"Not bad!" Norma says with enthusiasm. Despite everything, I have never seen her less than pleasant. "We're putting the wheels on Coda tomorrow."

"Already?" Clara exclaims.

"We're really pleased. We'll have that little robot on her way in no time."

"That's wonderful," I say and I really mean it, even though it is bittersweet. After Coda is gone, this will all end. The money has truly run out this time.

And even if there was somehow more, or if the team decided to continue on their own, the infrastructure isn't there, either. No one is building more rockets. And the fuel, well, that's all but impossible to come by. The necessary parts were left over from before, and the team has saved and hoarded and traded so we could do this. The resources are there to send Coda. But no more.

We have lost so much. And some of it, perhaps most of it, is just as well. There was so much that was wrong.

And a rover is just an object, a fancy vehicle.

It has been the privilege of a lifetime to be a part of this. To have this carved out space of, if not plenty, then at least enough for us to complete our project. Most have not been so fortunate as us.

I know Coda doesn't matter the way a person matters.But she has become, not merely a part of our lives, but central to it, the focus of everything we do here. I will miss her when she goes. I don't quite know what is next for me, most of us don't.

There aren't a lot of other jobs around here anymore.

I've lived in the little house on the edge of the woods my whole life, born there, grew up there. I've never left. Maybe I would have, if Mom hadn't died when I was finishing high school. Maybe I would have wanted space, a certain amount of independence. But I had more than enough as it was.

I know what it is like to be alone. Like Coda will be alone, on a brand new planet, with some old relatives who live far away and don't say much anymore and who you don't know anyway.

∽ • ∾

As I bike home from work that night, I can't shake the thought that we have all been putting everything that we have into the little robot who will leave us and mark the end of active space exploration.

Coda will send back data and there will be a small team to eagerly receive it, pore over it, delicately manipulate it. Hopefully, there will be something for us to learn, but it will not inform the direction of future research. Because there will be no future research.

When I was little, my mom often said that there had always been conflict and pain, but there had been a time when there had been more to life than suffering.

Now it seems like all we have are these very small shared moments, like Coda.

The rest of the world batters us, relentlessly. So far this year we have had snow for the first time in thirty-five years, followed weeks later by temperatures over 40C. Many of the local crops failed as a result, making food not just more expensive, but not readily available, either.

And it isn't only food, it's whole types of things that we used to be able to buy that just aren't there anymore—anything mass produced, from clothes to electronics to stationery.

I'm glad for the garden and that I don't feel the need to have a great deal, but the sense of precariousness remains.

Within all of this, Coda has been our focus.

This one last, small robot who can escape on our behalf.

∽ • ∾

I'm focusing on my breath, sinking into the elements that swirl around me, as I cycle home and I pass a woman on a bike pulling a trailer with a small child in it.

The child waves at me with the dinosaur they are holding.

Small toys—dolls and action figures, animals and vehicles, blocks—they pull me away from my breath and remind me of Agnieszka. She would join me while I was playing, something my mother rarely did, and would enchant the toys, one or two at a time.

The action figures would walk and jump and dance, the boats and rockets flying and spinning. The blocks tumbled, one over the other to form teetering towers. Animals would scurry and chase each other or hop on my shoulder.

I loved my mother, I did, but Agnieszka brought something very different into our lives, something delightful.

As much as I enjoyed it all, I didn't think very highly of Agnieszka's 'fun magic' when I returned to studying my path, shortly after my mom died. I thought of it as party tricks compared to the deep, meaningful inner work I believed I was doing.

∽ • ∾

We've pushed a bunch of tables together in the middle of the lunch room so that all of us can eat together, the whole team.

We are mere days away from the launch and the room swirls with feelings of excitement and loss.

Norma is the one who starts the speeches. "I feel I have given Coda the gift of energy, of being able to take herself wherever she needs to go."

The reaction is a mixture of nods and chuckles. Then Gil says, "Yes, I designed the wheels that will carry her to those places."

"I suppose I have given her a sense of curiosity, of investigation," says Lav, who developed the on-board sample testing system.

They continue, one after the other.

When it comes to my turn, I say "I provided Coda a clean space in which to grow."

It feels such a small contribution compared to the others, even though it is necessary.

I give my head a mental shake.

I am a witch. Perhaps there is something substantive I can contribute after all.

∽ • ∾

That night, as I'm biking home, I can't stop thinking about what I could actually do. The others have all contributed so specifically, so importantly, to Coda.

And I know that keeping her room clean, keeping the whole building tidy, these are important contributions.

I do know that. I'm not dismissing what I have done.

But it doesn't quite feel like enough.

This thought tangles with my feelings about Coda, about her leaving.

As my legs move faster and the wind ruffles my hair, a memory pushes at the edges of my mind, about Agnieszka and her books and her spells.

I couldn't have built Coda, but maybe I can give her something else.

The boxes are stored in the small room off the landing, in between floors, that Agnieszka used as her own while she lived with my mom and I.

I had never opened them. They arrived, unexpected if not entirely unwelcome, a year or two after my mom died. A short letter accompanied them.

Agnieszka was dead, too. Hit by a car while biking home from work one night.

The letter said that she wanted me to have her books.

It was a lot to absorb on top of my mom's death, especially since I had been wondering how she was doing since Mom died. I vaguely considered trying to find her, but hesitated because she had shown no interest in staying in touch with me.

I had stared at the boxes, not knowing if I wanted to throw the books at the walls or carefully return them to the shelves they had once occupied. Why had Agnieszka wanted me to have them? What had she wanted me to do? Feelings of anger, loss, and confusion I could not sort through crowded my mind.

So the boxes went into the room, which hadn't been used since she left anyway.

Closing my eyes, even now, I can picture how the room looked when she lived with us. Rows upon rows of books with worn edges and well-used spines, a full shelf occupied by the journals Agnieszka documented her work in, exploring what worked and what had not, ideas for improvement.

Now the room was dusty and stuffy, the shelves lining the walls empty. The middle of the room occupied only by the stacks of boxes.

I take a deep breath, the betrayal I felt after Agnieszka left still lurking. She did leave these books to me. It must have meant something.

I must have meant something.

Carefully, I open the box closest to me, trying not to dislodge the dust too forcefully. I pull out one book and then another.

This box does not seem to contain Agnieszka's notebooks but some of the other books I remembered from her shelves—*When God was a Woman, The Spiral Dance, The Great Cosmic Mother*. Their pages are yellowed and brittle and I touch them as little as I can, quickly ascertaining that none of the notebooks are underneath.

I push the box aside and pull forward the next one.

There I find the notebooks.

Sitting down on the floor, unmindful of the dust, I pull out one after another, looking for the cover I remember, stacking them on the floor around me as I do so.

And then there it is, the green and purple geometric patterns on the cover, the gold-edged pages. Opening it, I find Agnieszka's own hand, delicate and spidery, with small, enigmatic pictures decorating the margins of the pages.

I let my eyes rest on the writing for a long while.

I realize now how unfair I was to think of her magic as somehow lesser. Enchanting my toys was done, after all, for my sake. As was offering me comfort when no one else would. All out of her love for me, regardless of what came after.

Then I page through the book until I find "the comfort of a friend."

I read and re-read the instructions, to make sure it was what I intended, what I recalled.

∾ • ∾

Tomorrow Coda will be wrapped up and taken to the hangar adjacent to the launch pad, so she can be loaded in the nose cone.

There is only tonight.

I creep along the hallway I usually stride down. Technically, I have not broken into the building, as I have used my own keys, but I also don't have a work-related reason for being here.

As usual, I have very carefully ensconced myself, head to toe, in sterile garments.

I have committed the ritual to memory, because it is not the sort of ritual I normally undertake, but I have brought Agnieszka's book, too.

Just in case.

"Hello, Coda," I say as I slip into her room.

She is sitting there, still and dark, and for a moment I feel foolish.

She can't feel anything, she doesn't need me to do this.

I take a deep breath.

I'm here now, so I might as well go ahead.

I cast a circle around Coda, speaking softly as I do so and hold the firm intention in my mind to do no harm.

Then I sit with her, my hand on the side of her body, just above her front right wheel, as I remember Agnieszka and I sitting together, her hand on my shoulder, as she spoke the words from the book.

Those words are in my mind now and I speak them to Coda.

I will miss her, but now we are bound together, the two of us, as she leaves us on her adventure.

∽ • ∾

The remaining staff are standing in groups on a low hill, watching the rocket launch from the prescribed distance.

Me and Clara and Norma and Lav. We keep looking at each other, none of us able to suppress our grins.

As much as this is an end, it is a beginning for Coda.

While I consider the shiny white fairings hiding her, I accept that I have no idea whether my spell has been successful or not, or whether it matters.

Is there a part of me accompanying Coda to Mars?

Perhaps.

We have all put everything we had into wishing her into existence.

People talk about putting their heart and soul into all sorts of inanimate creations, but what if we really could?

Maybe it is enough to believe that she holds within her some aspect of our collective wish.

$\infty \cdot \infty$

Coda's mastcam rotates slowly, taking in the vast dusty expanse surrounding her.

From her location, on Solis Planum, she can see none of her forebearers—no rovers or landers, none of the remains of the missions that failed to successfully execute a landing.

She does not know if any of them remain operational. That knowledge is missing from her internal database.

The people who made her, who lovingly bestowed upon her the ability to see and hear, to examine and prognosticate, are hundreds of millions of kilometers away.

Regardless of Edie's intervention, a sigh is beyond the parameters of Coda's equipment.

Instead, she has developed a plan—where she will go and what she will look for. Yearning is also beyond her capacity, but as a word it would apply nicely to her in-built wish for adventure.

But there is also a small, round, warm feeling that she imagines to be between her x-band radio transponder and her multi-mission radioisotope thermoelectric generator. It reassures her that her people from Earth are, somehow, with her still. And it encourages her to find the others with whom she shares a common past.

She cannot articulate why, but it is not a need for their company so much as it is a wish to share with them the sense of comfort that she has been gifted.

AUDREY'S FLYING BICYCLE

✄ *G.J. Craddock* ∾

Audrey had decided quite early on in her witching career that, while very aesthetically pleasing and wonderfully traditional, a broom, even one that could fly, was not a practical or comfortable mode of transport.

A bicycle, with its wheels and its basket and its comfortable padded seat, now that, that was a transport for the practical and slightly daring witch.

So, Audrey had brought herself a bicycle, and after some trial and error made it fly, and in doing so thought herself very clever. Thought herself genius, and revolutionary, and all those things that one thinks of oneself when they have solved a problem that no one else has noticed.

Suddenly, with her little cart hooked to the back of her bicycle, she could carry whatever she wanted, wherever she wanted, in the height of comfort, metal frame rattling merrily.

To say that Audrey was terribly proud was to understate how far her metaphorical chest was puffed out over her creation.

Audrey landed her bicycle with a performative flourish at the next coven meeting, which received absolutely no attention from the happily chattering witches.

Gathered outside a tavern that had been generously donated to the host witch for the event, they seemed far too busy catching up on gossip, the weather, and other such conversational staples to appreciate the arrival of Audrey's bicycle.

Letting out a wistful sigh, Audrey parked her bicycle beside the rest of the brooms and made her way toward the gathered witches.

"You're always complaining, Clementine. Just do a few trips like the rest of us," one young witch was saying as Audrey approached the group.

Audrey knew that voice. It was Carol, and Carol was the type to treat tradition as gospel. She hadn't been overly impressed with Audrey's bicycle idea.

The witch that was being spoken to, Clementine, let out a deep sigh and curled a finger around her hair, as if the very idea was exhausting her.

It was beautiful hair, Audrey noticed. All golden ringlets, artfully pulled up into a tousled bun that made Clementine look attractively disorganised.

"Oh, I know, but it is such a long way to go once, let alone twice. The broom does get mighty uncomfortable on long trips."

"What's happening?" Audrey asked, never one to wait for an invitation before opening her mouth.

"Oh, Clementine is moving out of her cottage and having trouble balancing everything on her broom," Carol said, smirking conspiratorially as if Audrey would find this as pathetic as she did.

"My bike could do it," Audrey proclaimed.

"You haven't even finished your bike!" Carol said, demonstrating that she had been paying more attention than Audrey had previously thought.

"Have so. Rode it here today," Audrey retorted, standing tall and puffing out her chest. "Far more comfortable than a broom, just as I predicted."

Clementine put a hand on Audrey's shoulder, and Audrey felt her brain fuzz at the edges with the contact.

"Does it have a cart?" Clementine asked.

Clementine was much too close. "A what?"

"Your bicycle?"' Clementine said, smiling in a way that made Audrey's toes curl.

"Sure does," Audrey said.

Beside her, Carol was scowling at the resting hand, like a dog whose bone was being tampered with. Audrey ignored her occasional nemesis and sometimes friend.

"Are you sure it'll work, Audrey?" Carol asked, trying to poke a hole in Audrey's slowly inflating ego.

Audrey was having none of it. "Yes!"

"In one trip?" Carol said.

"In one trip," Audrey confirmed, doubling down.

Clementine had a sparkle in her eyes that Audrey would have found a little troubling, if she had been feeling at all level-headed.

"With your cart?" Clementine asked.

"With my cart! It'll be easy."

Clementine hooked her arm through Audrey's with a happy chirp and smiled up at her. "Oh, thank you, this has been stressing me so."

On Audrey's other side Carol was bright red and looked ready to spit on Clementine.

"No problem," Audrey said vaguely, her head full of bicycles and 'arm.'

∽ • ∾

Audrey arrived at Clementine's cottage the next day.

Clementine's now-former residence was an opulent cottage located in the far corner of a duke's well-manicured and sprawling gardens. Audrey's mouth had dropped open at the ostentatious wealth of it, and was still open as she landed and rolled her bicycle towards the cottage.

It was the kind of cottage you dreamed of living in as a child, with creamy white walls, brown bricks, and roses curling over everything.

A pile of very fancy looking suitcases sat on the cottage's front steps.

The front door opened to reveal Clementine. She had pushed the door open with a hip, as her arms were full of the most warded traveling case that Audrey had ever seen or felt.

Glyphs and sigils coated the outside of the case, and even a meter away Audrey could feel the little hole in the magic where the case should have been.

"What under the moon is in that?" Audrey asked, kicking down her bicycle stand and walking up to peer at the suitcase.

"Nothing worth worrying about," Clementine said, adding it to the top of the pile. "Did you bring your cart?"

"Sure did!" Audrey said, always happy to be distracted by questions about her bicycle. "I used a weightless spell on it and then attached a direction commandment between the bike and the–"

"Great," Clementine said in the glazed tones of someone who had both stopped understanding and stopped listening.

". . . cart," Audrey trailed off. "I'll just start loading up, shall I?"

Most of the suitcases were heavy enough that Audrey could only move one at a time. She was glad that she had gone with the weightless spell, instead of the standard flying one.

"What's all the warding against anyway?" Audrey asked, keen to keep the conversation going as she stacked the last of the suitcases in her cart.

"Something is looking for what's inside. I'd prefer they didn't find it," Clementine said shortly, as she added the case under discussion to the top of the pile.

Audrey's mind flooded with questions, but the whooshing sound of a broom overhead saved her from having to choose between them.

Audrey and Clementine looked up to see Carol's broom spiralling towards them from above.

"What are you doing here?" Audrey asked, stalking up to Carol as she landed. Carol pulled up her flying goggles and smirked in a way that made Audrey's blood boil.

"You didn't think I'd just believe you?" Carol said.

Audrey found she couldn't actually think of an argument against that.

"Well, don't get in my way," she said, stalking back to her bicycle. Carol trailed behind, broom slung over her shoulder, radiating smugness.

Audrey started to tie the suitcases down as Carol peered at the bicycle.

"What the hell is in that, Clementine?" Carol asked, staring at the suitcase balanced on the top of the pile. One end was slowly being pushed down by the straps as Audrey tightened them around the load.

Clementine, who was climbing onto her broom, scowled at Carol and threw the cottage key onto the steps. "None of your business, Carol. Now let's go, I don't want to be here any longer than necessary."

Not waiting for either of them to mount, Clementine swooped up into the sky.

Audrey poked her tongue out at Carol with glee. Nothing quite made her day like pushing Carol's buttons. "Yeah Carol, none of your business."

She swung her leg over the bicycle and swooped up into the sky as well.

"Clementine isn't as nice as she looks, you moron!" Carol shouted behind her.

Audrey ignored the warning and instead focused on the wind rushing in her ears as she gained loft, the sound of the cart rattling comfortingly behind her.

She levelled out as she reached the same altitude as Clementine, who hadn't stopped to wait for them. Instead, she'd headed out across the hills to the west, her figure silhouetted against the blue sky.

"What the hell is she keeping in this case anyway?" Carol's disgruntled voice came from somewhere near Audrey's trailer. The question was followed by the click of a suitcase being opened.

"Carol! You can't just go through people's stuff!" Audrey shouted, scandalized, peering ahead to see if Clementine had noticed the invasion of her privacy.

"There's a dragon egg in here," Carol said, as if she couldn't quite believe it.

"What?!" Audrey said, scandalized again, but for different reasons. "Who would be stupid enough to take a dragons egg?"

"Clementine, apparently."

There was a scuffling sound, and Audrey turned her head just in time to see Carol hovering above the cart, dangling awkwardly to scoop the egg out of the case for Audrey to see.

The egg was about the size of Audrey's head, and was speckled in a way that would have made it vanish in a landscape of brown rocks.

"Put it back, Carol! You can't just take peoples stuff!" Audrey hissed, looking to see if Clementine had noticed.

"Clementine clearly did," Carol snapped back, and before Audrey could retort, shot off to catch up with Clementine, egg tucked under her arm.

"Carol! Damn it!" Audrey shouted, spun her pedals once, and chased after Carol.

"What the hell is this, Clementine?!" Carol shouted, once the pair were in range. "Are you trying to get us killed?!" She waved the egg to emphasize her point.

"Why are you two going through my stuff?!" screeched Clementine, almost leaping off her broom with rage.

"I didn't! It was all Carol!" Audrey said, pulling up beside the two egg thieves. "I would never go through anyone's stuff."

"You didn't answer my question. Are you suicidal? I knew you'd made some dumb choices before, but this is something else, Clementine." Carol's voice was scathing.

"I thought it would make a good familiar, all right? Imagine the power!" Clementine said, hunching defensively.

"A familiar?!" yowled Carol and Audrey at the same time. The thought of someone turning something as powerful and wild as a dragon into an overly entitled pet was almost too foreign of an idea for Audrey to hold in her head.

"That would never work," Carol said, laughing.

"It might if I raised it from a hatchling. Now give it back," Clementine said, and made a snatch for the egg.

Carol, who already had the egg precariously balanced, lurched back to avoid it being taken from her. The egg wobbled, balanced on the tips of her fingers.

All three watched in horror as the egg wobbled one way, and then the other, and then finally tipped into empty space.

"You idiot!" Clementine and Carol shouted at each other, both reaching for the egg, and both missing.

"I've got it! I've got it!" Audrey shouted, and dove for the plummeting egg. If nothing else, this surely would make them appreciate her bike.

It was a close thing. Cart rattling like every negative thought she'd ever had, Audrey raced against gravity, hands outstretched.

For a moment, heart trying to climb out of her mouth, Audrey thought she'd misjudged the angle of her dive, and that the egg and the tiny dragon growing inside would splatter somewhere far below.

The two paths crossed. Her hands brushed and then grasped the smooth surface. She held the egg above her head like a trophy.

"I got it!" she shouted and looped her bicycle so that she was heading back towards the two other witches. "I got– oh shit."

A massive burst of flame took her eyebrows off.

Looming above all three of them, like the angriest mother that had ever been, was a dragon.

"This is why I have the warding, you idiots!" Clementine screeched, beating at the now burning tail of her broomstick.

Carol, desperately doing the same thing, just screamed.

As the dragon grew closer, the scale of its size began to be petrifyingly apparent.

What flies were to Audrey, the witches were to the dragon. The egg, now clutched in Audrey's sweating hands, was the size of her head, and the dragon's scales were the size of her.

Audrey could not believe that something so huge had come out of an egg so comparatively tiny.

The dragon roared again and a burst of flame spilled out high, the bright reds and oranges stark against the blue of the sky.

Clementine, whose broom was still burning, spiralled down and away, sweeping under Carol, and then under Audrey, as if she intended to use both as shields against the dragon's rage.

This left Carol, still patting away at her broom, staring down the dragon's maw.

"Oh fuck," Carol said, looking up. The dragon opened its mouth again, revealing rows of teeth, and a gaping cavern as dry as the inside of an oven.

There was a sucking sensation as the dragon took a deep breath. Audrey could feel herself being dragged, just slightly, toward the dragon.

Audrey realized that it was getting ready to breathe fire again, fanning its inner flame with an in-rush of air.

Audrey also realized that, while Carol could be annoying, she could also be rather good fun, and Audrey would really prefer not to see her get turned into soot right before her eyes.

She held up the egg. Held it as high as she could, almost on tippy toes, as she balanced on the bicycle pedals.

"Oi! Over here! I've got what you're looking for!" Audrey shouted, loud as her lungs would allow.

It must have been loud enough, because the maw snapped closed, and the head turned so that a single great eye could stare at Audrey and the egg she was holding.

The moment the dragon focused on her, Audrey sat back in her seat and shot up into the sky, heading away from Carol, Clementine, and the dragon.

She could feel the dragon behind her, huge flaps of wind that she felt more than heard.

Audrey levelled out once she was clear of her fellow witches, and the dragon pulled level with her, the two facing each other across the wide blue sky.

There was a rushing sensation again as the dragon began sucking in air.

Audrey didn't wait for it to finish. Placing the egg in the basket attached to the front of her bike, she spun the pedals once, twice, three times and pushed her bike toward the dragon and leapt clear, praying to all the magic she knew that Clementine would catch her as she fell.

The flames shot over her head, singeing the trailing tips of her hair. Wind rushed in her ears, and she simultaneously felt that she wanted to puke, and that her stomach had been left somewhere far above.

This was, Audrey decided, the stupidest thing she had ever done for a pretty face. She shut her eyes and tried not to think about anything else.

There was a jolt and suddenly she wasn't falling anymore.

The hands holding her waist gripped tighter as Audrey's stomach caught up with her and she leant over the side of the broom to puke into the wide blue yonder. A hand came up to pull what was left of her hair out of the way, just in time.

Wiping the corners of her mouth, she opened her eyes and looked up, hoping to see golden curls.

She was disappointed. Carol was looking at her with part awe and part annoyance. She blushed and let go of Audrey's hair.

Maybe severe black and a pointed nose had its own charms, Audrey considered.

"That was my stuff, Audrey! How could you!" Clementine swooped in beside them, her hair frazzled and her broom still burning.

There was a whoosh, and all three looked up to see the dragon flying above and past them, one giant claw curled delicately around the tiny egg.

Falling past the dragon was a smoking speck of grey.

"Carol! My bicycle!" Audrey shouted, her throat burning from the acid of her puke.

The metal frame was still intact, rattling in the sky as it plummeted towards the earth, the cart trailing behind like a wobbling tail, Clementine's suitcases smoking. The fancy red fabric that Audrey had coated the seat and handlebars with was an ashy mess.

"It's still intact," Carol said, her voice filled with so much disbelief that Audrey had to smile smugly.

Carol dove for the bicycle. As they pulled even with the rapidly descending bicycle, Audrey, not having pushed her luck far enough, jumped.

She landed awkwardly on the bicycle seat, her crotch stinging from the impact. A desperate swing of her foot set the pedals spinning.

For a moment she thought the magic would not take. That it had been burned away. That this time she really would plummet to her death.

A second that seemed to go on forever, and then there was a thrum as the magic came back, and the bike bobbed instead of falling. Audrey threw her arms in the air and let out a crow of success.

Clementine and Carol floated down beside her, Carol looking slightly frazzled and Clementine pale with relief.

"Oh, thank goodness my stuff survived."

Audrey grinned a little less and Carol rolled her eyes.

The trip across the mountains was uneventful after that, although Audrey dreaded to think about what could happen that would be worse than an angry dragon.

Clementine's new residence was perched on the top of a dramatic cliff face and looked like a castle that someone had shrunk.

Between Carol and Audrey, the cart was quickly emptied.

The three of them stared down at the pile of singed suitcases on the steps.

"Well thanks for losing my dragon egg and getting my stuff burnt," Clementine said with a level of sarcasm that seemed to impress even Carol, going by her raised eyebrows.

"Always happy to lend my bicycle to a good cause," Audrey said, still impressed that it had survived a confrontation with a dragon, and feeling like that deserved some more recognition.

Clementine sniffed, and, golden curls bouncing, began to drag her stuff inside, ignoring the two other witches now that her needs had been met.

Audrey watched her sadly, the reality of the moment not meshing with her inner vision.

"I was impressed."

"What?" Audrey said, turning to look at Carol who was standing beside her.

"I was impressed with your bicycle. My broom was almost in cinders." Carol's cheeks were bright red and she was looking anywhere that wasn't Audrey's face. "If you wanted to run over the spells with me, I'd be interested."

"Really?" Audrey said, feeling like she could float away.

"Yeah," Carol said, and then quicker than Audrey could blink she kissed her on the cheek and shot up into the sky, flame-damaged broomstick vanishing past the horizon.

Audrey touched her cheek and stared up into the sky.

Maybe today hadn't been so bad after all.

CONTRIBUTORS

A. P. Howell holds a master's degree in history and her jobs have spanned the alphabet from archivist to webmaster. Her short fiction has appeared in places like *Daily Science Fiction*, *Little Blue Marble*, *Translunar Travelers Lounge*, *Underland Arcana*, *ParSec*, *Martian: The Magazine of Science Fiction Drabbles*, *Community of Magic Pens* (Atthis Arts), *In Somnio: A Collection of Modern Gothic Horror* (Tenebrous Press), and *Darkness Blooms* (The Dread Machine). She lives with her spouse and two kids, tweets into the void @APHowell, and keeps a website at aphowell.com

ↅ • ↄ

Emily Burton (she/her) is a queer author and editor with recent publications in *Columbia Journal*, *Stonecoast Review*, and *Miracle Monocle*. Her story, "Old Goliath," first appeared in the Autumn 2021 edition of *Capsule Stories*. Emily can be reached at eburtonoliver@gmail.com

ↅ • ↄ

Ether Nepenthes (they/them) is a queer, non-binary, disabled, neurodivergent writer hailing from the south of France. Their main occupations are writing relatable, heartwarming stories and keeping up their reputation as the friendly neighbourhood cryptid. You can find a complete list of their publications on their website www.ethernepenthes.com and-slash-or get in touch on Twitter @queer_of_swords

ↅ • ↄ

G.J. Craddock is a writer and illustrator who consumes far too many ice lattes. She lives in fear of spiders gaining human level intelligence and then choosing violence. You can find her on Instagram/ Twitter @gjcraddock. One day she will build a website.

ↅ • ↄ

Gretchin Lair is deeply affected by unkindness, especially in alternative communities. She is a Leo who was surprised to learn about sidereal time. You can contact her at gretchin@scarletstarstudios.com

ↅ • ↄ

Hester Dade is a queer autistic writer and illustrator based in the UK. Inspired by modernity, nature and where the two meet. Their bike has a hand-painted basket and has survived adventures with cars, a deer, and a particularly inquisitive fox. They have several short stories, poems, and non-fiction pieces published, a full list is available at www.hesterdade.com.

ᗡ • ᗞ

Kathleen Jowitt writes across a range of genres, exploring themes of identity, redemption, faith, and politics. Her work has been shortlisted for the Exeter Novel Prize, the Selfies Award, and the Betty Trask Prize. Find her at www.kathleenjowitt.com.

ᗡ • ᗞ

M. Lopes da Silva (she/they/he) is a non-binary and bisexual author from Los Angeles. They write queer California horror and everything else. Their horror has been published or forthcoming in *The Dead Inside*, *Stories of the Eye*, and *Your Body is Not Your Body: A New Weird Anthology to Benefit Trans Youth in Texas*. Dread Stone Press will be publishing their first novelette *What Ate the Angels*—a queer vore sludgefest that travels beneath the streets of Los Angeles—as Volume 2 in their new Split series.

ᗡ • ᗞ

M. A. Blanchard's fiction has appeared in *PseudoPod*, *Prairie Fire*, *Canthius*, *Dark Matter Magazine*, and more. A linguist by training and a surrealist by inclination, she curates the #sfstoryoftheday on Twitter @inquisitrix and writes a column on short speculative fiction for *Fusion Fragment*. Find her on the web at mablanchard.com

ᗡ • ᗞ

Mohini Hirve is an engineer and organizer based in Massachusetts. They like to write and think about the intersection of abolition, queerness, and disability through the lens of speculative fiction. Their poetry has been published in MIT's *Rune Magazine*.

ᗡ • ᗞ

Monique Cuillerier is a lesbian writer living in Ottawa (Canada) who enjoys space, cats, politics, and gardening (but not necessarily in that order). She and her work can be found at notwhereilive.ca

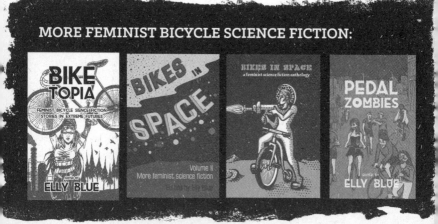